A Christmas Cruise Caper

A Short Christmas Story

By

Judith Keim

BOOKS BY JUDITH KEIM

THE HARTWELL WOMEN SERIES:
The Talking Tree – 1
Sweet Talk – 2
Straight Talk – 3
Baby Talk – 4
The Hartwell Women – Boxed Set

THE BEACH HOUSE HOTEL SERIES:
Breakfast at The Beach House Hotel – 1
Lunch at The Beach House Hotel – 2
Dinner at The Beach House Hotel – 3
Christmas at The Beach House Hotel – 4
Margaritas at The Beach House Hotel – 5
Dessert at The Beach House Hotel – 6
Coffee at The Beach House Hotel – 7 (2023)
High Tea at The Beach House Hotel – 8 (2024)

THE FAT FRIDAYS GROUP:
Fat Fridays – 1
Sassy Saturdays – 2
Secret Sundays – 3

THE SALTY KEY INN SERIES:
Finding Me – 1
Finding My Way – 2
Finding Love – 3
Finding Family – 4
The Salty Key Inn Series – Boxed Set

SEASHELL COTTAGE BOOKS:
A Christmas Star
Change of Heart
A Summer of Surprises
A Road Trip to Remember
The Beach Babes

THE CHANDLER HILL INN SERIES:
Going Home – 1
Coming Home – 2
Home at Last – 3
The Chandler Hill Inn Series – Boxed Set

THE DESERT SAGE INN SERIES:
The Desert Flowers – Rose – 1
The Desert Flowers – Lily – 2
The Desert Flowers – Willow – 3
The Desert Flowers – Mistletoe & Holly – 4

SOUL SISTERS AT CEDAR MOUNTAIN LODGE:
Christmas Sisters – Anthology
Christmas Kisses
Christmas Castles
Christmas Stories – Soul Sisters Anthology
Christmas Joy
The Christmas Joy Boxed Set – (2023)

THE SANDERLING COVE INN SERIES:
Waves of Hope
Sandy Wishes
Salty Kisses

THE LILAC LAKE INN SERIES

Love by Design – (2023)
Love Between the Lines – (2024)
Love Under the Stars – (2024)

OTHER BOOKS:

The ABC's of Living With a Dachshund
Once Upon a Friendship – Anthology
Winning BIG – a little love story for all ages
Holiday Hopes – A Christmas Novella
The Winning Tickets – (2023)

For more information: **www.judithkeim.com**

PRAISE FOR JUDITH KEIM'S NOVELS

THE BEACH HOUSE HOTEL SERIES – Books 1 – 6:

"Love the characters in this series. This series was my first introduction to Judith Keim. She is now one of my favorites. Looking forward to reading more of her books."

BREAKFAST AT THE BEACH HOUSE HOTEL is an easy, delightful read that offers romance, family relationships, and strong women learning to be stronger. Real life situations filter through the pages. Enjoy!"

LUNCH AT THE BEACH HOUSE HOTEL – "This series is such a joy to read. You feel you are actually living with them. Can't wait to read the latest one."

DINNER AT THE BEACH HOUSE HOTEL – "A Terrific Read! As usual, Judith Keim did it again. Enjoyed immensely. Continue writing such pleasantly reading books for all of us readers."

CHRISTMAS AT THE BEACH HOUSE HOTEL – "Not Just Another Christmas Novel. This is book number four in the series and my introduction to Judith Keim's writing. I wasn't disappointed. The characters are dimensional and engaging. The plot is well crafted and advances at a pleasing pace. The Florida location is interesting and warming. It was a delight to read a romance novel with mature female protagonists. Ann and Rhoda have life experiences that enrich the story. It's a clever book about friends and extended family. Buy copies for your book group pals and enjoy this seasonal read."

MARGARITAS AT THE BEACH HOUSE HOTEL – "What a wonderful series. I absolutely loved this book and can't wait for the next book to come out. There was even suspense in it. Thanks Judith for the great stories."

"Overall, Margaritas at the Beach House Hotel is another wonderful addition to the series. Judith Keim takes the reader on a journey told through the voices of these amazing characters we have all come to love through the years! I truly cannot stress enough how good this book is, and I hope you enjoy it as much as I have!"

THE HARTWELL WOMEN SERIES – Books 1 – 4:
"This was an EXCELLENT series. When I discovered Judith Keim, I read all of her books back to back. I thoroughly enjoyed the women Keim has written about. They are believable and you want to just jump into their lives and be their friends! I can't wait for any upcoming books!"

"I fell into Judith Keim's Hartwell Women series and have read & enjoyed all of her books in every series. Each centers around a strong & interesting woman character and their family interaction. Good reads that leave you wanting more."

THE FAT FRIDAYS GROUP – Books 1 – 3:
"Excellent story line for each character, and an insightful representation of situations which deal with some of the contemporary issues women are faced with today."

"I love this author's books. Her characters and their lives are realistic. The power of women's friendships is a common and beautiful theme that is threaded throughout this story."

THE SALTY KEY INN SERIES – Books 1 – 4:
FINDING ME – "I thoroughly enjoyed the first book in this series and cannot wait for the others! The characters are endearing with the same struggles we all encounter. The setting makes me feel like I am a guest at The Salty Key Inn...relaxed, happy & light-hearted! The men are yummy

and the women strong. You can't get better than that! Happy Reading!"

FINDING MY WAY- "Loved the family dynamics as well as uncertain emotions of dating and falling in love. Appreciated the morals and strength of parenting throughout. Just couldn't put this book down."

FINDING LOVE – "I waited for this book because the first two was such good reads. This one didn't disappoint.... Judith Keim always puts substance into her books. This book was no different, I learned about PTSD, accepting oneself, there is always going to be problems but stick it out and make it work. Just the way life is. In some ways a lot like my life. Judith is right, it needs another book and I will definitely be reading it. Hope you choose to read this series, you will get so much out of it."

FINDING FAMILY – "Completing this series is like eating the last chip. Love Judith's writing, and her female characters are always smart, strong, vulnerable to life and love experiences."

"This was a refreshing book. Bringing the heart and soul of the family to us."

THE CHANDLER HILL INN SERIES – Books 1 – 3:

GOING HOME – "I absolutely could not put this book down. Started at night and read late into the middle of the night. As a child of the '60s, the Vietnam war was front and center so this resonated with me. All the characters in the book were so well developed that the reader felt like they were friends of the family."

"I was completely immersed in this book, with the beautiful descriptive writing, and the authors' way of bringing her characters to life. I felt like I was right inside her story."

COMING HOME – "Coming Home is a winner. The characters are well-developed, nuanced and likable. Enjoyed the vineyard setting, learning about wine growing and seeing the challenges Cami faces in running and growing a business. I look forward to the next book in this series!"

"Coming Home was such a wonderful story. The author has such a gift for getting the reader right to the heart of things."

HOME AT LAST – "In this wonderful conclusion, to a heartfelt and emotional trilogy set in Oregon's stunning wine country, Judith Keim has tied up the Chandler Hill series with the perfect bow."

"Overall, this is truly a wonderful addition to the Chandler Hill Inn series. Judith Keim definitely knows how to perfectly weave together a beautiful and heartfelt story."

"The storyline has some beautiful scenes along with family drama. Judith Keim has created characters with interactions that are believable and some of the subjects the story deals with are poignant."

SEASHELL COTTAGE BOOKS:

A CHRISTMAS STAR – "Love, laughter, sadness, great food, and hope for the future, all in one book. It doesn't get any better than this stunning read."

"A Christmas Star is a heartwarming Christmas story featuring endearing characters. So many Christmas books are set in snowbound places...it was a nice change to read a Christmas story that takes place on a warm sandy beach!" Susan Peterson

CHANGE OF HEART – "CHANGE OF HEART is the summer read we've all been waiting for. Judith Keim is a master at creating fascinating characters that are simply irresistible. Her stories leave you with a big smile on your face and a heart bursting with love."

~Kellie Coates Gilbert, author of the popular Sun Valley Series

A SUMMER OF SURPRISES – "The story is filled with a roller coaster of emotions and self-discovery. Finding love again and rebuilding family relationships."

"Ms. Keim uses this book as an amazing platform to show that with hard emotional work, belief in yourself and love, the scars of abuse can be conquered. It in no way preaches, it's a lovely story with a happy ending."

"The character development was excellent. I felt I knew these people my whole life. The story development was very well thought out I was drawn [in] from the beginning."

A ROAD TRIP TO REMEMBER – "I LOVED this book! Love the character development, the fun, the challenges and the ending. My favorite books are about strong, competent women finding their own path to success and happiness and this is a winner. It's one of those books you just can't put down."

"The characters are so real that they jump off the page. Such a fun, HAPPY book at the perfect time. It will lift your spirits and even remind you of your own grandmother. Spirited and hopeful Aggie gets a second chance at love and she takes the steering wheel and drives straight for it."

THE DESERT SAGE INN SERIES – Books 1 – 4:

THE DESERT FLOWERS – ROSE – "The Desert Flowers - Rose, is the first book in the new series by Judith Keim. I always look forward to new books by Judith Keim, and this one is definitely a wonderful way to begin The Desert Sage Inn Series!"

"In this first of a series, we see each woman come into her own and view new beginnings even as they must take this tearful journey as they slowly lose a dear friend. This is a very well written book with well-developed and likable main characters. It was interesting and enlightening as the first portion of this saga unfolded. I very much enjoyed this book and I do recommend it"

"Judith Keim is one of those authors that you can always depend on to give you a great story with fantastic characters. I'm excited to know that she is writing a new series and after reading book 1 in the series, I can't wait to read the rest of the books."!

THE DESERT FLOWERS – LILY – "The second book in the Desert Flowers series is just as wonderful as the first. Judith Keim is a brilliant storyteller. Her characters are truly lovely and people that you want to be friends with as soon as you start reading. Judith Keim is not afraid to weave real life conflict and loss into her stories. I loved reading Lily's story and can't wait for Willow's!

"The Desert Flowers Lily is the second book in The Desert Sage Inn Series by author Judith Keim. When I read the first book in the series, The Desert Flowers-Rose, I knew this series would exceed all of my expectations and then some. Judith Keim is an amazing author, and this series is a testament to her writing skills and her ability to completely draw a reader into the world of her characters."

THE DESERT FLOWERS – WILLOW – "The feelings of love, joy, happiness, friendship, family and the pain of loss are deeply felt by Willow Sanchez and her two cohorts Rose and Lily. The Desert Flowers met because of their deep feelings for Alec Thurston, a man who touched their lives in different ways."

"Once again, Judith Keim has written the story of a strong, competent, confident and independent woman. Willow, like Rose and Lily can handle tough situations. All *the characters are written so that the reader gets to know them but not all the characters will give the reader warm and fuzzy feelings."*

"The story is well written and from the start you will be pulled in. There is enough backstory that a reader can start here but I assure you, you'll want to learn more. There is an ocean of emotions that will make you smile, cringe, tear up or outright cry. I loved this book as I loved books one and two. I am thrilled that the Desert Flowers story will continue. I highly recommend this book to anyone who enjoys books with strong women."

A Christmas Cruise Caper

A Short Christmas Story

By

Judith Keim

Wild Quail Publishing

A Christmas Cruise Caper is a work of fiction. Names, characters, places, public or private institutions, corporations, towns, and incidents are the product of the author's imagination or are used fictitiously. Any resemblance to actual events, locales, or persons, living or dead, is coincidental.

No part of *A Christmas Cruise Caper* may be reproduced or transmitted in any form or by any electronic or mechanical means, including information storage and retrieval systems, without permission in writing from the author, except by a reviewer who may quote brief passages in a review. This book may not be resold or uploaded for distribution to others. For permissions contact the author directly via electronic mail:

wildquail.pub@gmail.com
www.judithkeim.com

Published in the United States of America by:

Wild Quail Publishing
PO Box 171332
Boise, ID 83717-1332

ISBN# 978-1-959529-59-0
Copyright ©2023, Judith Keim

Dedication

This story is for those who believe in a little Christmas magic.

PROLOGUE

STARR

On this mid-November evening, Starr Snowden sat in her apartment filled with determination. She would NOT spend another Christmas like last year with everyone hugging her, telling her how sorry they were, that another man, better than Reggie Bellingham, would see how wonderful she was. Dear Reggie had dumped her the week before Christmas, leaving her with her worst Christmas holiday ever. This year she planned to be as far away from Ellenton, New York, as possible.

Starr picked up the brochures she'd been given by a sweet woman at a local travel agency and carried them to the couch in her apartment. It was time to get serious.

She looked with envy at the information about cruises and sighed. With her teacher's salary, there was no way she could afford a cruise, even if a Christmas cruise would be perfect timing. She was about to toss the latest cruise brochure aside when a picture of an elf caught her attention. The ship *Tropical Promise* was offering a special Christmas Cruise with Santa and his two elves. Below the announcement was a tiny paragraph that offered a free trip to anyone willing to play the part of Santa's elf. It gave an online link for those interested and instructed them to fill out a lengthy questionnaire.

At the idea, a mixture of anticipation and dread filled her. She worked with first graders all day. She knew how excited, how wild, they could be before Christmas. Why torture herself by dressing up as an elf and dealing with them and their over-anxious parents? Still, it was a chance to get away.

Her cell phone rang. *Parker Culbert.*

Starr smiled. She and Parker had been best friends since first grade when Parker's family moved next door. Of all the people she knew, Parker would give her a straight answer.

"Hi, Starr. I know you're dreading the holidays. I thought I'd check to see how you're doing."

"Thanks. I admit the thought of spending another Christmas in town is depressing. I stopped at the travel agency downtown to get some ideas of what I could do, and I've learned about a fantastic opportunity."

"Oh? Tell me. Hurry before the baby wakes and I have to get dinner on the table."

Starr gave Parker the details.

"Oh, Starr! Do you know what I would give to be able to do something like that? You know I'm happily married and I love my baby girl, but to be away in the sun and warmth and able to sleep through the night would make it the best Christmas ever."

"As you know, I don't have those problems. In fact, it's been feeling pretty quiet at home now that my beloved cat is gone."

"I know, sweetie. And look, before you hear it from anyone else, I think you should know Reggie and his bride have just announced they're pregnant."

Starr refused to let the angry words in her mind escape her. She was so tired of enduring the details of Reggie's life without her.

"I'm sorry, but I thought you should know," said Parker. "It's better to hear it from me than from someone else."

"Yes, thank you. I wouldn't want to be blindsided with that news without the privacy you're allowing me. This gives me a little time to get prepared to face my family. I know they care, but it's all too much."

"Maybe you should go ahead and apply for that cruise job. It sounds terrific. Oops, gotta go. The baby is crying."

Starr ended the call and sighed. It was her move, and she was going to make it count. Before she could change her mind, she went to her computer and began to fill out the required information, including answering the question about why she wanted to get away.

NOAH

On this early December evening, Noah Jordan ended the call with his mother and held his cell phone in his hand filled with the urge to throw it through his office window. Glum, he stood and stared out at the view of Boston below. He loved his mother, but she had a crazy idea that this was the Christmas he should ask Cynthia Withers to be his wife. He supposed Cynthia would make some man happy; it just wasn't him. His mother and hers had been pushing them together for years. The perfect match, they thought, even though Cynthia had been secretly seeing another man. Something he would never tell his mother or hers. He'd backed out of any serious dating with Cynthia when one of his friends told him about it. He wasn't a social guy, anyway. He was happiest working on logarithms and other technical matters and away from the need to make small talk at stuffy cocktail parties and the like.

Noah's best friend and business partner, Chip Caldwell, walked into his office. "What's gotten into you? I can hear you growling through the wall."

"It's my mother. She's determined I ask Cynthia Withers to be my wife, and I'm even more determined not to. I've talked to Cynthia, and she agrees. Neither her mother nor mine know she's dating someone her family wouldn't approve of." He shook his head. "I want to skip Christmas here in Boston. I can't take another year of disappointing my family."

"C'mon. It's been a long day. Let's go to Johnny's for a beer and talk. Maybe we'll come up with an idea for you. You can't get trapped like that. Besides, you told me you didn't want to get married when we're busy getting our company going."

"Right. That's what I think. Who wants to be tied down at this stage?"

Chip shuffled his feet on the carpet and looked up at Noah with an expression that screamed of betrayal. "I need to be honest with you. I'm giving Jenna a ring on Christmas Day. Unlike you, we've been planning to get married ever since I met her at one of your mother's parties two years ago."

"Don't think my mother hasn't brought that up, traitor!" said Noah. "But I'm happy for you. Jenna is a sweet woman, perfect for you, and I wouldn't want our work to mess up your relationship with her. I don't intend to get married for years. It's been pushed on me for a long time. Too long."

"Understood. Now, let's go get that drink."

Noah grabbed his cell and his wallet and followed his best friend out of his office into the financial district of "Bean Town." He liked his life and wasn't about to change it. And though he worked long hours, he loved his job.

When he and Chip walked into the bar, Noah let out a huge sigh of relief at finally being able to relax. It had been a long week with a new client pressing for an update on a project Noah had been working on. The job sounded simpler than it was—a new program that detected fraudulent information from investors who were anxious to participate in any project opportunities. Numbers were numbers. But information didn't always add up. It was his job to find out what underlying data were fake. Sure, you could surmise some information had been taken from social media and other sources, but the trick was to be able to determine which pieces of information reported were real.

Noah sat beside Chip at the bar. The inside of Johnny's was like many other sports-themed bars with wood-paneled walls and numerous big-screen televisions. But it was a neighborhood bar in an area full of movers and shakers in the financial world. Information gathered there was always interesting.

The bartenders knew everyone and were clever enough to remember names. One of the younger bartenders approached them. "Hey Chip! Noah! Two IPAs?"

Ignoring the Christmas music playing quietly on the speakers, Noah grinned, and nodded.

The bartender left and quickly returned with two foaming mugs of ale. He leaned against the counter. "So, what do you two have planned for the Christmas holidays? Going somewhere? Skiing? The Caribbean?"

"I wish," grumbled Noah. "I need to get out of town."

"Woman trouble?" the bartender asked.

Noah took a sip of his ale and licked the foam off his lips. "You could say that. Woman and mother trouble. My mother is pushing for me to get engaged to a girl I'm *not* about to marry."

"Hm-m-m. One of those situations. If you really want to get away, I've got some news that might help you. One of my friends was telling me about a cool opportunity for a single guy. It sounds kinda corny, but it could be a lot of fun. He can't go, after all, and is looking for someone to replace him."

"What are you talking about?" Chip asked.

The bartender leaned forward. "He was able to get a free 7-day cruise in the Caribbean over Christmas. The only catch? He has to play Santa Claus for the first part of the trip."

Noah looked at Chip and grinned. "I'm ready to do most anything to get out of another bad family holiday."

Chip clapped him on the back. "Sounds like this is the

perfect excuse to escape. By telling your mother you're doing someone a favor and helping little kids enjoy Christmas, what can she say?"

Noah chuckled and turned to the bartender. "How do I get hold of your friend?"

He waved a man over to them. "This is Jake Barton. Jake, Noah Jordan here. He might be interested in taking over for you on the Christmas cruise."

"Hey, man, that would be great," said Jake, shaking Noah's hand. "I hate to back out of the trip, but I have a family emergency and can't go. I haven't told the cruise company yet, but now I can, as long as you'll replace me." Jake filled him in on some of the details, and it all sounded fine.

Chip elbowed him. "What have you got to lose? Take it before it goes to someone else."

Noah hesitated, thinking of his mother, and then remembered their conversation earlier this evening. "Okay. Deal." He held out his hand and Jake shook it.

"Give me your information and I'll text you the form I had to fill out. Thanks. You can honestly tell your family you're doing me and my family a huge favor."

They exchanged phone numbers and conversed for a while to find out more about one another. Jake seemed like a straight-up guy, and by the time they got through talking, Noah was pleased with the idea of going on a Christmas cruise, even if he did have to wear a Santa costume for part of the trip.

CHAPTER ONE
STARR

With Thanksgiving behind her, thankfully, Starr trudged up the stairs to her apartment in downtown Ellenton holding the mail in her hand. She'd seen the envelope from Caribbean Cruises and realized her whole life depended upon getting accepted as one of Santa's elves.

People were kind and caring, but if she had to listen to one more person telling her about the baby her ex, Reggie, and his wife were having, she'd have to move away. Why was her life so off-kilter? How could one man do this to her?

She set down her purse, flung off her down jacket, and picked up the envelope. Staring at it, she said a little prayer that it would be good news.

Carefully, she opened the envelope and unfolded the paper inside. She closed her eyes, took a deep breath, and then stared at the typewritten words.

"Congratulations! Welcome Aboard! You've been selected to be one of Santa's elves for our special Christmas Cruise leaving Miami on December 22nd. In addition to providing you with room and board and costuming, we will offer you a small stipend and free transportation from the airport to the ship's berth in Port Everglades. By the way, your name, Starr, is perfect as our first chosen elf."

Starr couldn't help herself. All her disappointment over the past year erupted in sobs that shook her body. She'd been so low, so unsure of herself, so humiliated by all that had happened to her. Maybe now, she'd be the best darn elf the *Tropical Promise* ship had ever seen. She had to do something to prove to herself that she was worth something.

She picked up her cell and called Parker with the news.

"I'm delighted for you. It's going to be just the break you need," gushed her friend.

"In truth, I need this more than I realized," said Starr. "Now, I have to make sure I can still fit into my summer clothes. This cold, miserable weather always tempts me to nibble between meals."

"You're fine just as you are," countered Parker. "And if you need to borrow any clothes, you're welcome to whatever I have. If I can't go on a cruise, at least my clothes can."

They laughed together, but Starr's mind was racing. Maybe it was time to go thrifting or take a trip into the city for some winter cruise sales.

She and Parker chatted for a few minutes more, and then Starr ended the call and rushed to her closet. Though she couldn't afford to spend a lot of money on clothes, she always held out for quality over quantity, and at times like this, it paid off.

After trying on summer clothes and vowing not to gain an ounce, Starr set aside several outfits she could wear on the cruise when she wasn't dressed up like an elf. After all, the cruise was for only seven days. After she got off the ship, Starr intended to stay in Miami for New Year's Eve. She'd already looked into Airbnb offers and was hoping to find a single room somewhere. If worse came to worst, she could always splurge and stay in a low-cost hotel. One thing was certain, she would not be in Ellenton to welcome the new year. She had to do better than that.

###

For the next few weeks, Starr was too busy to worry about the cruise. Now that she had a flight to and from Ft. Lauderdale, and she had her clothing sorted out with only one dress borrowed from Parker, she was ready to get her little students through the days until Christmas.

Their eyes rounded with delight at the colorful decorations the art teacher helped them make. Storytime was even more exciting. In addition to some traditional books, Starr shared stories of Hanukkah and Kwanzaa, which tripled the joy of the season. At this young age, her students were very open about different customs in celebrating the holidays, and she vowed to keep that same openness on the ship. She'd be a Christmas elf, but that didn't mean she couldn't celebrate in other ways too.

As she sat in her classroom one afternoon after her students had left for the day, Starr wondered if this was what her life would be going forward, devoting herself to other people's little ones, helping them to learn and to grow more independent. In cold weather like this, just making sure each child was dressed appropriately for going outside was a major undertaking.

Whenever the thought of Reggie and his cruel unfaithfulness threatened to break her down, she remembered she would not be in town for the holidays and would miss all the family fussing that was sure to take place. Even though her mother thought Starr was being selfish for taking off, she was trying her best to understand why Starr wouldn't be with them.

When at last, the children left her classroom for the holiday vacation, and she was straightening her room, fresh excitement filled her. It was really going to happen. The cruise line had sent her information about picking her up at the airport and gave her instructions on where to go at Port

Everglades. Getting on the ship could take a while, she was told, so she'd have to be patient. She'd be treated no differently from any other passenger, though she'd embark a day earlier than they.

At home, she went through her items to pack one more time. Parker had lent her a gorgeous, strapless black cocktail dress that would serve her well for New Year's Eve, wherever she might end up. She'd tried it on, and with her dark-red hair and green eyes, the dress seemed made for her. Though she wasn't tall, her curves filled out the simple dress nicely. Her black, high-heel strappy shoes would be perfect with it.

Starr studied the dark-blue bikini that still fit her and decided if she needed another, she could get one in Florida before the cruise, or perhaps at one of the shops on the cruise. She'd memorized the itinerary. They'd leave from Ft. Lauderdale to go to George Town, Grand Cayman, to Cozumel, Mexico, to Nassau in the Bahamas and back to Ft. Lauderdale. A perfect little jaunt to prepare for New Year's Eve.

Her cell rang. *Her mother.*

Starr held in a groan and clicked on the call. "Hi, Mom! How are you?"

"Frankly, I'm still disappointed you won't be with the family for Christmas. Even Aunt Jo, who adores you, thinks it's foolish for you to try and make an escape. You can't let Reggie chase you away from your family. We love you and want you to be part of Christmas like always."

"Mom, even if I wanted to change my mind, which I don't, it's too late to back out now. I can't let the children or their families down on this cruise. They've signed up to see Santa and his elves. It's part of the package."

"I knew you'd say that," sighed her mother. "I'll hold your Christmas gifts here, and after you come home, we'll have a special dinner with you so you can open them."

"Thanks, Mom. That'll be nice. I'll send you a post card from Mexico." A thrill of excitement coursed through Starr as she said the words. She wouldn't be in Cozumel for long, but after this trip, she could at least say she'd been to Mexico.

"Okay, dear. Your father and I hope you have a fantastic trip. Safe travels."

Starr clicked off the call knowing how lucky she was to have such understanding parents. Someday she hoped to be as loving to children of her own. But at the moment, the thought of even dating was enough to give her nerves a nauseating jangle.

CHAPTER TWO
NOAH

Noah looked up from his work as Chip came into the office. "Aren't you done yet? It's getting late, and it's almost time for you to leave for the airport."

"Okay. I'm ready. Be sure and call me if anything comes up that needs my attention."

He closed his computer, put it in his carryon bag, and stood. "Have a great Christmas. Good luck with Jenna. I'm sure she'll be thrilled with the ring. It's a beauty."

They gave one another bro hugs, and Noah raced from his office to the elevators. He was told that though the ship sailed on the 22nd, he needed to be aboard the ship on the 21st. That was fine with him.

His cell phone rang. *His mother.* He let it go. He'd call from the gate.

It had started to sleet in Boston. As he exited onto the street in Post Office Square, he lucked out when a cab pulled up in front of the building. The cabbie's passenger exited the car and Noah slid into the back. "I need to go to Logan Airport. Terminal B. How's the tunnel?"

"Not too bad for this time of day. Where are you going?" the cab driver asked.

"Ft. Lauderdale, where I hope the weather is better than this," said Noah. His mother might be disappointed he wasn't going to be with her and his brother and family, but the thought of sun, warmth, and palm trees was enticing. He'd make it up to his mother somehow.

###

Once he got through security, Noah headed directly for the gate. He was cutting it short but had enough time to make it. Luckily, he was traveling first class and could easily board the plane without a hassle.

At the gate, boarding was delayed. Noah took advantage of the time to phone his mother.

"Hi, Mom. You called. I'm at the airport about to leave. If I don't get the chance to speak to you for a while, I want to wish you a Merry Christmas. Thanks for understanding that I needed to change things up a bit."

"No problem," said her mother cheerfully. "I think you're right and we do need to change things up a bit, as you say. I'll speak to you later. Safe flight, darling."

"Thanks, Mom," said Noah, surprised his mother hadn't mentioned her disappointment as she usually did ever since he'd made the announcement about the cruise.

More relaxed now, he boarded the plane feeling better about his decision. He loved his family, but it was time to be alone. His brother, Rob, and his wife, Tara, had four-year-old twin boys, Austin and Henry. Two handsome little troublemakers. What one didn't think to do, the other did, causing one challenge after another. Noah's mother adored them. Thanks to Rob and Tara, she'd have a busy Christmas without him.

He stowed his luggage in the rack above him, relieved not to have to pack too much—shipboard clothes and a suit for a New Year's Eve party a client was giving in Miami Beach. When he heard Noah was going to be in the area, he'd insisted on Noah attending it. Noah agreed to it, not caring if he had a date or not.

As he took a seat, a flight attendant asked if he wanted a drink. "Great. How about a beer?"

The flight attendant smiled, letting her look linger with

interest. Noah was used to it. Though he didn't like to dwell on it, he knew he was good-looking.

The attendant returned with his beer and asked, "What are you doing in Florida?"

"Going on a Christmas cruise," he answered, unwilling to tell her he'd be dressed as Santa Claus. At the time, it had seemed a funny joke. Now, he wasn't so sure. But he'd made a promise to Jake and the cruise company, and he'd honor it.

Once the plane was in the air, Noah leaned back against the cushion and closed his eyes. The typical end-of-the-year rush was always exhausting. Chip would handle most of it now that the main work was done.

Sometime later, the pilot's voice came on over the loudspeaker. "Ladies and gentlemen, we're about to land. You're in for some beautiful Florida weather for the holidays. Enjoy."

Sitting up, glancing out the window, Noah saw the blue sky and below, palm trees and the ocean. Excitement filled him. Maybe this trip was just what he needed. He'd been so busy with work that he'd missed socializing with friends.

The shuttle bus driver pulled the vehicle to a stop at the Port Everglades Terminal 26. The seaport in Fort Lauderdale was enormous with a lot of different functioning areas. Noah grabbed his suitcase and headed inside, following the signs to where a line of people, mostly workers for the ship, he guessed, were waiting to be checked through to where they'd embark. Tomorrow, the passengers would come aboard.

Noah showed his proof of citizenship, had his picture taken, and was issued an ID card, charge card, and stateroom key. As he boarded the ship, he was met by a crew member who directed him to his cabin on one of the lower levels in the bow of the ship.

"You're lucky you get a single room," said the crew member, a trim, gray-haired man who looked several years older. "Most performers have double cabins and must share. I believe the two Christmas elves are already here."

"Okay, thanks," said Noah, thinking how lucky he was. With a name like Noah, it had seemed only logical that he'd be paired with someone, like the animals on the famous ark.

CHAPTER THREE
STARR

When Starr walked into the cabin she'd been assigned, a young blond woman was unpacking her things. The closet door was open, and in a glance, Starr could see how little room was left for her things.

"Hi, I'm Starr Snowden," she said smiling at her roommate.

The blonde turned around. "Hey, I'm Vianna Skinner. Are you the other elf?"

"Yes, I am." Starr studied the buxom woman of medium height and gazed at the makeup that covered her face, thinking she looked like a wannabe starlet with those long fake eyelashes. "Is this a role you won?"

She tossed her long, blond hair over her shoulder and formed a pout. "No, the captain, Herbert Brockman, is my uncle. I convinced him I'd do a great job because I'm taking acting lessons. He was supposed to give me a private cabin, but here I am with you."

"I see," said Starr, telling herself this job was for only seven days and she could get through most anything. "I don't have any fancy clothes except for a couple of dresses. Please leave room for me to hang them up."

"I'm hoping we don't have to spend too much time with the kids. I want to meet some single, rich guys. It can't be all families aboard this ship."

"We have to be ready to help anytime we're asked," said Starr. "The crew member who greeted me as I came aboard told me that tomorrow we elves will be welcoming people on board the ship for most of the day."

"Well, I might have to welcome them aboard on the Lido deck. That's where all the action takes place. Especially when we are about to get underway," said Vianna. "I don't want to miss out on any of it."

Starr kept quiet as she hung up her two dresses and unpacked the rest of her things into the drawers in the built-in bedside table beside the twin bed Vianna had left for her to use. She hoped tomorrow would be better. Until Christmas morning, her time was not her own, and like it or not, she'd be sharing a lot of it with Vianna.

She wondered who was playing Santa Claus. She had yet to see an older, heavy-set man who looked right for the part.

After getting settled in her cabin, she and Vianna left it.

"I'm going to take a tour of the ship, so I know where everything is," said Starr, picking up the map of the ship she'd been handed.

"I'll see you later. I'm going to the Lido Deck and get a drink," Vianna said before walking away with a swing to her stride.

Starr studied the map. There were thirteen decks. Decks 3 and 4 held a large theater. A spa was located on Decks 11 and 12. Beyond that, the ship was loaded with pools and provided one activity after another, and several private restaurants. It really was a city on the waves, she thought.

She'd read that the pool or Lido deck was where sailaway parties were held. She decided to go check it out for herself. Even if she had to be dressed in an elf costume, she wanted to be there when the ship departed. This was her first and possibly only cruise, and she didn't want to miss that magical moment.

She went to the lobby area first. She knew that on Christmas Eve, Santa and his elves would be delivering cookies and gifts to specific staterooms that had requested the service and wanted to get acquainted with the various sleeping areas while the ship was so empty.

It was almost an hour later when Starr made it to the pool deck. Several food and snack bars were there, along with some serving alcoholic drinks. Feeling the need to celebrate, she went over to a cute little outlet where tropical drinks were being offered.

Almost giddy, Starr bought a fruit and rum drink in a reusable souvenir glass and carried it toward a collection of tables lining a portion of the port rail.

Vianna waved and called to her. "Over here."

Starr hesitated and then walked to her, intent on making an effort to get along.

As she approached, she got a look at the man sitting at the table with Vianna. He had chestnut hair that gleamed in the sun and when he lifted his sunglasses, his light-blue eyes were startling. As he stood to greet her, she realized how tall he was.

"Hey, Vianna says you're the other elf. I'm Noah Jordan, better known as Santa Claus for the next few days."

She smiled and shook the hand he'd offered her. "Hi. I'm Starr Snowden."

He held a chair for her. "Have a seat. Vianna and I have been talking about our duties. We're going to be busy until Christmas morning. Then we can take a break and enjoy the rest of the cruise, even if it's for only a couple of days."

"Yes, I've studied the itinerary, and I'm okay with it. I'm just glad to be away from New York and the cold weather there," she said.

"Yeah, me too. That, and family issues," said Noah.

"I know that all too well," Starr said, turning as Vianna got to her feet.

"I'm going to wonder around and see who else is on board," Vianna said.

"Good luck," said Starr, and explained to Noah, "Vianna's looking for rich single guys."

"Hmmm, how about you? Is that why you signed up for this?" His eyes, mostly hidden behind his sunglasses still had a way of boring into her.

"Absolutely not," said Starr with a firmness no one could mistake. "The last thing on my mind is finding a man, rich or otherwise. In fact, that's why I'm here. I can't go through another Christmas holiday with my family feeling sorry for me because my ex-boyfriend dumped me over a year ago and is now expecting a baby with his bride."

"Wow! That's a lot to handle," said Noah.

Starr clapped a hand over her mouth and shook her head. "Sorry. I didn't mean to say all that. I guess I just needed to get it out there, so there's no misunderstanding about me."

Noah gave her a friendly smile. "I'm glad you mentioned it because I'm in the same sort of situation of not wanting to get involved. My mother thinks I should marry someone I have no interest in. To be honest, I'm escaping my family for the holidays. My brother and his wife have twin boys who are four, and that should keep my mother busy."

"Okay then. That's settled. We can be friends helping each other out to get through the holidays."

"What do you do when you're not escaping?" Noah said.

Starr chuckled. "I'm a first-grade teacher. It's why I'm here. I know how excited kids get at this time of year, whether it's Hanukkah, Kwanzaa, or Christmas. I confess, I debated whether to take a complete break from kids or do this elf role, but I couldn't resist a chance for a cruise."

"I found out about this from a friend of a friend," Noah explained. "He was set to come and had to cancel because of family issues. He was very happy I was willing to take over for him."

"What do you do for a living?" Starr asked him.

"I work in IT ... research. I was able to get away because of the holidays."

"Nice," she commented, though she had the feeling he was holding something back. She let it go. This was an escape for them both.

Vianna returned. "No luck so far. But the passengers aren't even aboard." She sat down next to Noah and nudged his arm. "Too bad you're not rich."

His cheeks grew pink. "You got that right. Why else would I be doing something like this? Right?"

CHAPTER FOUR
NOAH

Noah sat at the table with Vianna and Starr wondering how two women could be so different. Vianna was a stunner but as shallow as they come. And Starr? With her wavy, soft red hair, and button nose with freckles sprinkled across it, Starr was ... cute. Wholesome. Nice. In fact, she reminded him of Jenna, Chip's girlfriend.

He'd been surprised to hear Vianna complain about having to share a cabin and realized again how fortunate he was to have a cabin alone, even if it was in the bowels of the ship.

He checked his watch. "We're supposed to meet the cruise director in the lobby soon. I'll walk you to it."

"The lobby is called the atrium aboard a ship," said Vianna, flashing her false eyelashes at him.

"How is it you know so much about cruising?" he asked.

"My uncle is Captain Brockman. My family and I have been on board before. In fact, that's how I got the job. I know this ship, and a little nepotism doesn't hurt."

"Well, at least you're honest about it," said Noah getting to his feet.

They walked together to the atrium and found several people gathered around a small woman with brown hair in braids. She was wearing a navy skirt, a crisp white blouse, and white boat shoes. She noticed them and waved them over.

"Hi! Glad you could join us. I'm Julia Crawford, your cruise director. Or in your case, your boss." Smiling and talking at the same time, she seemed perfect for her job. Her enthusiasm made up for her size, and he couldn't help the grin that crossed his face. He had a feeling this Santa thing might be more fun than he thought.

The two women introduced themselves, and then he shook hands with Julia and told her and the group of fellow workers his name.

"Welcome aboard. After our meeting about the ship's rules, I'll take the three of you to the room where you'll be expected to change into and out of your costumes and show you where you will be sitting with the kids here in the atrium for story time as well as for Santa's visiting hours. I have it organized, so all you have to do is appear at the proper place at the proper time for your activities."

Vianna raised her hand. "Will we have plenty of free time too?"

"Oh, yes," Julia said. "Especially in the evenings. After Christmas morning, you'll be totally on your own."

"That will be nice," said Vianna with a satisfied nod.

Julia raised a finger of warning. "Tomorrow, however, will be a busy time for you. You two elves will be greeting passengers as they arrive."

"What about Santa Claus?" Vianna asked. "What's he going to do while we're working?"

"He'll make an appearance in all the dining rooms at the evening meal. That's when he'll be busy."

Noah exchanged a smile with Starr. This was really happening.

Later, struggling to put his wig and beard in place, Noah's enthusiasm waned. It was going to be a lot of work. The good thing was, no one would be able to recognize him under all this white hair covering his own hair and most of his facial features. He patted the round, stuffed stomach attached to his frame. Whoever had designed the costume had done a great job. Except for his young, unblemished, strong hands, he looked the part. And he'd cover them with white gloves.

Starr approached him. "You're looking real, Santa!"

He laughed and studied her in her costume. She wore a red blouse, green vest, and short green skirt over what looked like red and white striped tights. Red felt booties covered her feet. Her red curls were hidden in part by a green felt hat whose long point folded down and was kept in place by a silver bell. She looked...well ... adorable.

"I had no idea I'd be forced to wear something like this," grumbled Vianna. "I'm going to speak to my uncle about it."

"I think it's too late," said Starr. "We have a busy day ahead of us tomorrow."

Vianna whipped her hat off. "Well, tonight, I'm going to party while I can."

She went back behind the changing screen.

Noah shrugged and shook his head. This whole scene was something he hadn't thought out that well, but he'd stick with his promise and do his job.

Starr gave him a little wave. "See you on the Lido deck?"

"Sounds like a plan." Being able to relax after doing his duty just might get him through the job at hand.

That evening, Noah sat with Starr and a couple of other people recruited to provide a special Christmas for their passengers, including an older married couple who put on puppet shows. They explained that they'd written something special for this cruise.

Intrigued, Noah thought he'd tape some for his nephews. They might like it.

"Can I get you something?" he asked Starr.

"A glass of red wine would be nice, thanks. I'll share my

nachos with you until it's time for our crew buffet."

"Deal. I'm hungry and I hear the crew food is very good even if we eat separately from the passengers."

Noah returned to the table with a glass of wine for Starr and handed it to her. "Enjoy!"

He sat down and a moment later shifted his chair closer to Starr's to allow another person to move a chair into the circle at the table. His bare leg touched Starr's thigh and he felt a flash of sensation course through him. He glanced at her, but Starr didn't seem to notice the surprising attraction he'd experienced.

He took a sip of his beer and leaned in to hear the conversation going on about Christmas celebrations for the crew.

CHAPTER FIVE
STARR

*N*o-o-o! Starr froze for a mini-second, looked away from Noah, and pretended to study the wine in its glass. She'd felt a jolt when Noah's leg touched the skin on her thigh and she would not, could not afford to go there. This was to be a fun cruise away from the mess at home with no sexual interactions with any male. She was still too emotionally raw from her ordeal with Reggie, and she didn't want to be like Vianna, hunting down a man. This time was to be used for having fun with the kids and determining if she wanted to stay in Ellenton. Lately, she'd begun to think it might be nice to move away. Not so far she couldn't easily visit family and friends, but with enough distance to give her a fresh start.

The rest of the evening went well, and when Starr tucked herself into bed, she gripped her pillow with a welcome sigh. The people she'd met were an interesting, friendly group and would be a source of fun during the time away.

She saw Vianna's bed was still covered with the clothing she'd tried on and discarded and wondered when Vianna would appear. Unwilling to wait for her, Starr turned off the light and rolled on her side. Tomorrow was going to be a long day.

Starr's alarm went off at seven. She immediately sat up and stretched. She and Vianna were to be ready by ten o'clock to become part of the welcoming group to receive passengers. She wanted time to have a decent breakfast and maybe take a stroll around the deck before getting into costume.

Vianna's head whipped around. "Oh, God! What time is it?"

"Seven. Time to get up if you want breakfast and a break before we start our jobs. When did you get in?"

"Later than I thought," groaned Vianna. "I should've listened to you last night and come to bed when you did. Oh, well, if you're that enthusiastic about your job, you can help cover up for me."

"I'll see you later," said Starr. She had no desire to get mixed up in Vianna's mess.

The breakfast buffet set up in a different area from where the passengers were served was a delight filled with a lot of the same foods offered to them. Starr helped herself to cut-up fresh fruit and then, disregarding calories, chose pancakes, and a cup of black coffee.

As she went to find a seat, she noticed Noah and went over to his table. "Mind if I sit down?"

He smiled at her. "I'd enjoy the company." He studied her tray. "I had pancakes too. I'm glad you're not one of those women who doesn't dare eat what she really wants."

Starr grinned. "I'm on vacation. Of sorts."

He laughed. "Yeah, I'm wondering if I made a mistake by accepting this job. But it's only for a few days. I can put up with almost anything, and this is one Christmas I don't need to be with my family."

She took a sip of coffee and nodded. "I feel the same way."

After she finished her breakfast, Starr remained at the table with him talking about their jobs and the need for a break.

"Have you ever been to the islands?" she asked him.

"Yes, but I prefer to be there on my own than visiting on a cruise ship. Still, when I think of the weather back in Boston,

I'm happy to be here."

"Me, too," she said and checked her watch. "I have time to stroll along the main deck before I need to change into costume. I'll see you later."

"Okay. Next time you see me, I'll probably be in costume. In the meantime, I'm going to catch some sun rays at the pool."

Starr left him and went to the main deck. Looking down at the gathering crowd from the height of the ship, she realized how enormous the ship was and how many people would be aboard.

After she'd walked along the main deck in an effort to work off some of her breakfast, she hurried to the room designated as a changing room for performers and got into her costume. Though her legs and arms were covered along with the rest if her, some thoughtful person had made the costume with lightweight fabrics and materials.

She loved getting dressed up for Halloween, and staring at herself in the mirror, she couldn't stop a smile from spreading across her face. The kids were going to love meeting Santa and his elves.

At the appointed time, she met two staff members at the boarding site. Julia was there, of course, and smiled at her. "You look fantastic! Where's the other elf?"

"I don't know. I imagine she'll be here soon," said Starr.

Julia went over the procedure. She and another staff member would check passengers in, and if children were present, she and Vianna were supposed to say, "Welcome Aboard" and hand them each a gift bag of goodies.

"And if you're able to chat with them, that makes it even nicer for them," said Julia. "And if they ask for Santa, you can say he might be looking over the ship in another area or some such thing. Got it?"

Starr nodded. "Yes I'm a teacher."

"Right," said Julia grinning at her. Turning, a frown crossed her face. "Vianna, you're late, and please straighten your costume."

Vianna looked as hungover as she must have felt.

"Here. I'll help you," said Starr. She shifted the costume around, so it fit properly and adjusted Vianna's hat.

"Thanks," Vianna said softly. "I don't want my uncle to know about this."

"I'm not saying a word," said Starr with determination. She had enough family issues of her own.

"Okay, here we go!" said Julia, a cheerful tone ringing in her voice.

While not all passengers were traveling with children, many were. As Starr spoke to them, she tried to guess the children's names, making a game of it to help pass the time. But it was fun to be part of the excitement of passengers boarding with high hopes for a fabulous cruise.

For the most part, the kids were darling. A few were crabby from waiting in line and being over-anxious about the unknown. Starr spent a little extra time with them. On the opposite side of the aisle, Vianna seemed to be doing her part to help, though if a handsome man was in the line she tended to flirt until Julia spoke to her.

Starr gazed at the family walking the gangway toward them. It looked like a grandmother accompanying a young couple and two little boys. Because the boys were on Vianna's side, she spoke to them while Starr waited for three girls to approach with their parents.

After the bulk of passengers had arrived, Julia said, "Why don't the two of you take turns for the rest of the afternoon.

Most are on board, but people are allowed to board until it's time to depart."

Exhausted, Starr said, "I'd like to at least grab a bite to eat." She looked at Vianna.

"Go ahead. I'll take the first shift."

"Okay, Starr, you have an hour before you have to relieve Vianna," Julia announced.

Grateful, Starr headed for the staff cafeteria. On her way, she recognized a few of the families. When the children spied her and waved, she waved back and hurried away, thinking of the family her ex had started. More than ever, she was thrilled to be away from home.

Inside the cafeteria, she chose a chicken salad and iced tea for her lunch and sat down to eat it.

Noah walked in, saw her, and joined her. "How's it going being an elf?"

"It's exhausting, but I love seeing the excitement on the smaller kids' faces when they see me. It's going to be fun for you tonight when you walk around."

"I hope so. Are there a lot of children coming aboard?" he asked.

"Yes, some real cuties too. I'm not sure but I think I saw some twins. If not, they were brothers that looked a lot alike."

"You'd know it if they were twins. They just sort of fit together. My nephews are like that. Guess I'll go back to the pool."

"I'm going to my stateroom to freshen up. See you later."

CHAPTER SIX
NOAH

Noah was enjoying himself, using his free time to relax by the pool. It was especially sweet because he knew what it would be like if he'd stayed at home. His mother, as usual, would be driving everyone crazy with plans for Christmas Eve and Christmas Day in addition to her annual Christmas Party on the 23rd. The only satisfying thing that had come out of her parties recently was the relationship between Jenna and Chip.

He found an empty lounge chair and was about to sit down when he noticed a couple with an older woman and two small boys. He stared at them, rubbed his eyes, and studied them.

His heart pounded in his chest. Panic, like a bolt of lightning, shot through him. He had to come up with a plan. RIGHT NOW.

He left the pool deck and hurried down to his stateroom. If he was lucky, he could catch Starr before she went back to her welcome spot.

Still breathing heavily, trying to fill his lungs with air, he pounded on her door.

She opened it and stared at him. "What's wrong?"

"You know that family with two small boys who looked alike? They're mine. You've got to help me."

"Help you? Why?"

"It's my mother. As I told you earlier, I escaped my family to avoid any talk about an engagement to someone I have no desire to marry. I need you to cover for me as my girlfriend."

"Your girlfriend? You know I have no interest in getting involved with any man. I'm still too emotionally shaky from all that happened to me. I don't think I have it in me to even pretend to like you as a boyfriend. I already like you as a friend, but that's it."

"You have no idea how persistent my mother is. I'm surprised she didn't bring Cynthia with her. My time here is going to be unbearable if I don't get her off my back. I'll say that we met online and it's turning out great. How about that?"

Starr heard the pleading in his voice and hesitated.

"We said we'd be friends helping each other with the cruise. Remember? This is how you can help me. Don't worry, I promise once we end the cruise you won't ever have to see me again. I'll make up a story to my family about why we ended it. Right now, I can't be trapped on a boat for a week with my mother who will make it clear she's disappointed in me."

Starr's mind spun. Noah was her only friend on the boat. And like they'd said, they'd help one another out. Would it hurt to pretend to be his girlfriend? He'd made it clear he had no interest in her, was willing to never see her again after the cruise. She'd be safe with him. No promises to break.

He gripped her hand. "What do you say?"

"Okay. If I can pretend to be an elf, I guess I can pretend to be your girlfriend. Now, let's get a few facts settled."

"Thank you!" Noah gave her a quick hug and stepped back. "You've told me a little bit about your family and I know what you do for a living and some of your favorite things. But each time we're alone, you'll have to feed me more about yourself."

"And I know you do something in IT and live in Boston. What else?"

Noah shuffled his feet and looked down. When he lifted his face, his look was sheepish. "I don't just do something with IT. My best friend, Chip Caldwell, and I own a very successful computer company doing investigative work for corporations.

He's going to propose to his girlfriend, Jenna, over Christmas. Another reason my mother is eager for me to find a wife and settle down. If Chip can do it, so can I."

"You're just what Vianna is looking for," said Starr.

Noah gave her a horrified look. "No way do I want to get involved with her, even as a fake girlfriend."

Satisfied, Starr nodded. "Okay, we'll do this. But you'll owe me big time."

"We'll say we met on the dating app Forever Yours a couple of months ago. How's that?"

"All right. We can say we clicked and after talking to each other wanted to do something for the kids, that when I heard you'd signed up for Santa Claus, I signed up for work as an elf. It was a new bonding thing."

"Ah, that sounds believable. My family is all about a wife and husband sharing a partnership. That's how my parents were until my father died from a heart attack eight years ago."

"My parents are still alive and together and would agree that's how things work best between them." Starr checked her watch. "I've got to go back to work. You'll have to figure out the best way to handle your family. I'll do my best to go along with it. Okay?"

Noah hugged her. "You're the best. This Christmas Caper just might work. Thanks."

He stepped away, and Starr stood a moment telling herself the shivers she felt were just warnings to be strong. He had no idea how hard she fought her reactions to him.

When Noah went back to the pool deck, he found his brother and sister-in-law stretched out in lounge chairs. His mother sat on the pool's edge, watching his nephews play in the water.

"Well, look who's here!" Noah announced, approaching them with a forced note of excitement. "How did you manage this?"

His sister-in-law, Tara, sat up and smiled at him. "Surprise! When we heard about the cruise, we called and got last-minute accommodations. It's such a great idea and will keep the boys busy before Christmas."

Rob stood and embraced his brother in a bro hug. "Hope you don't mind. Thought you might like the distraction from facing Mom. She actually invited Cindy to join us, but Cindy got sick at the last minute and couldn't come."

His mother walked over to them. "We wanted to surprise you. You said it was time to change things up and I thought this was the perfect way to do it." She hugged Noah. "We all would've missed you if you'd been away without us. Love you, son."

"Love you, too," said Noah, meaning it even as their appearance frazzled him.

"Cynthia couldn't make it at the last minute, but she said she could join you at home for New Year's Eve," said his mother.

"Too bad that won't happen," said Noah.

"Why not?" His mother frowned.

Noah cleared his throat, swallowed, and then blurted, "Because I've got a girlfriend. She's here with me on the boat."

His mother's eyes widened. "That's a surprise. When do I get to meet her?"

"After we're through with our stint at dinnertime. She's an elf. We wanted to do something for kids this Christmas and have some fun together."

"Oh, my! She sounds interesting. What's her name?" asked his mother.

"Starr Snowden."

"How appropriate. Sounds a bit Christmas-y." His mother gave Noah a broad smile.

"I bet she's beautiful," said Tara, nudging him playfully.

"She's very cute," Noah said, bringing a look of surprise to the adults' faces. Cynthia was a tall, stunning woman. No one would call her cute.

Just then, Henry and Austin bombarded him, throwing their arms around his legs, their wet bathing suits soaking his skin.

"Uncle Noah! We didn't know you were here," said Austin.

"Santa Claus is coming on the cruise," Henry said. "Maybe you'll get to see him too."

Noah ruffled their wet, auburn hair. "Maybe. We'll see."

Austin tugged on his hand. "C'mon, into the pool."

"Okay, okay. Give me a few minutes to talk to your parents and I'll join you. Gran can watch you until then." Pleased he'd effectively given himself some time alone with Rob and Tara, Noah sent his nephews on their way. His mother followed.

As soon as the three of them were alone, Rob said, "What's really going on? Have you been holding out on us?"

"It's true we met very recently. Through a dating app, actually. Wait until you meet her. Starr is a wonderful person, a good friend."

"Friend?" Tara asked, narrowing her eyes at him.

"Isn't that what you're supposed to do? Choose someone you like to spend time with? Be friends first, then lovers?" Noah countered.

"Something's fishy," said Rob. "You go away and suddenly you have a girlfriend who you've kept hidden from everyone?"

Noah shuddered. Rob made it sound as if Starr was easy, someone after mere fun or after his money. She wasn't like that at all. "Listen, I know it sounds off, but please help me out by being accepting. Mom is going to be enough for us to handle. Can I count on you?"

Tara and Rob looked at one another and then turned to him.

"Don't make us regret this," said Tara. "You can't break your mother's heart."

Noah swallowed hard. "I won't." He was grateful Starr seemed such a genuinely sweet person. She'd know how to handle herself.

CHAPTER SEVEN
STARR

The entire time Starr was working during her shift greeting kids, she questioned whether she was crazy to have promised to help Noah. He was a nice man, and had been kind and attentive to her by offering to bring her wine, even standing as she was seated at a table with him. And to think he owned a *very* successful IT company meant he had money while she came from a much humbler background. Would his family reject her from the beginning? Her pride wouldn't let that happen.

When Vianna came to replace her, Julia said, "Okay, ladies. We're done. It's four o'clock and we'll need to get ready for the sailaway. You two can take the rest of the day off. Go to the Lido deck for the party."

When Starr got to the costume room, Noah was waiting for her.

"Hey, what are you doing here?" said Vianna. "You don't have to work for a couple more hours."

"I know. I'm here to see Starr."

Vianna raised her eyebrows and looked from him to Starr and back again. "You two got something going on?"

"As a matter of fact, we do," said Noah, placing an arm around Starr.

"Really? That was fast," Vianna said. "Well, I'm off to find a rich man."

"Go for it," said Noah shaking his head at her before turning to Starr. "I'm sorry I led you to believe I didn't have much money. I hope it won't make a difference to you that I do. I don't want my family to think that's why you're interested in me."

"If you really knew me, you'd know that money doesn't matter that much to me. I'm not ready to become involved with anyone, but when I eventually do, I want to meet a man who doesn't feel entitled because he's made money. I want someone to share a life with who's sincere, honest, and kind. Someone who's interested in me the way I am, not because he thinks he can change me to suit him."

"That sounds reasonable, logical," said Noah. "Now, you'd better tell me more about your family. I promised mine we'd meet them for the sail-away party."

"Okay, you know the basics—both parents alive and still married, hard-working middle-class people. One sister and one brother are both happily married. I'm the youngest by nine years. A surprise baby that everyone adored growing up, not that I was allowed to get away with much."

Noah gazed at her intently. "You already know about my brother, Rob, and his wife, Tara, and their twin boys. And you know that my father, Dean, died of a heart attack eight years ago. My mother, Sarah, still talks about him. She's turned her energy into charity work, socializing with friends, and adoring the twins. She's anxious for me to get married and settled down so she can have more grandchildren. Tara is unable to have more children. At first, Tara and my mother didn't always get along, but they're very close now. I've told Rob and Tara we met on a dating site recently."

"The Forever Yours dating app, right?

"Sure, that's fine. I'll say that Jenna, Chip's girlfriend, forced me to sign up," said Noah. "They know I'd never do this on my own."

"When did we actually meet?" asked Starr, unable to stop a nervous flow of energy through her. She hated lying, told her students how important it was to be truthful.

"Let's see. I went to New York for a business trip right before Thanksgiving. Why don't we say then? I was staying at The Manhattan at Times Square. We can mention seeing the sites together, make it seem romantic."

"You'd better do most of the talking. I haven't been in the city in a while and I certainly couldn't afford to stay at that hotel," Starr said.

"Okay. Just follow my lead." He gazed at her. "Let me know when you're ready by knocking on my door. We'll go up to the sail-away party together."

"Give me a few minutes," she said, wondering when she'd ever feel ready.

Noah took hold of her hand and led her through the throngs of people to where a nice-looking, gray-haired woman, wearing a silly pink paper party hat, stood beside two boys. The boys had bandanas tied around their heads like pirates and were bouncing on their feet with excitement while their grandmother held onto their hands.

Unexpected tears came to Starr's eyes. Her own grandmother, deceased now, was that type of grandmother, eager to please her grandchildren.

Nearby, a tall man with caramel-colored hair and a shorter plumpish woman with brown hair stood looking over the rail.

"There they are," Noah said. "Let's get this over with."

As they approached, the boys shouted, "Uncle Noah, look! The boat is going to move."

Just then a loud horn blast from the ship filled the air. They were underway! Starr could feel a smile spread across her face. She was actually on a cruise ship about to leave port.

Noah looked at her and winked, well aware of how excited she was.

She tugged him to the rail of the ship and they stood in the crowd as the ship pulled away from the dock. One of the twins looked up at her and said, "Is Uncle Noah going to marry you?"

Starr flashed a look at Noah and turned to the boy. "Your uncle and I just met. We're friends."

"Oh," the boy responded looking from her to Noah.

"What's going on?" asked Noah.

"I thought you were going to marry her," said the boy.

Noah gulped and lifted the boy's face. "Now, Henry, Starr and I are friends. If the time ever comes for something different, you'll be among the first to know. Okay?"

He nodded. "Gran's going to be sad."

In the stillness that followed, Noah's mother turned to them. "It's finally quiet enough for me to hear." She beamed at Starr, and Starr wished for a moment the scene she and Noah had created was real.

Noah's mother held out her hand. "Hello, I'm Sarah Jordan, Noah's mother."

Starr shook her hand while Noah said, "This is Starr Snowden." He gave Starr a broad smile, and she returned it.

"I'm very pleased to meet you," said Sarah. "We had no idea that Noah had a girlfriend and was keeping you a secret."

"Sometimes family doesn't need to know everything," said Noah. "Starr, you've already met Henry. Austin is his brother." He turned. "And here is mine. This is Rob and his wife, Tara."

Starr shook hands with them. Noah and his brother had the same straight nose as their mother and those light-blue eyes that were so arresting. Both had lanky builds, though Rob was taller.

Tara exuded warmth as she smiled at Starr. Her auburn hair, like her boys, and green eyes suited her round, pretty face. She put her arm around Austin and drew him close. Observing her, Starr could guess how sweet a mother she was.

"We came here to surprise Noah but have ended up more surprised than he," said Tara. "I hope these seven days at sea will give us a chance to really get to know you, Starr. Noah tells us you're an elf, that you decided to do something fun together for children at this time of year."

"Yes, I'm a first-grade teacher and understand how excited kids are at the holidays. Besides giving me ... us ... a chance to get away, our jobs give us the opportunity to do something nice to add to the joy of the season."

Noah wrapped his arm around Starr and pulled her close. "Isn't she special?"

"I want her to sit next to me at dinner," said Austin, giving her a cute, flirty smile that touched her.

"We won't be eating dinner with you for a few days. Maybe after Christmas," said Noah, tousling Austin's hair.

"But you might miss Santa Claus. He's going to visit us at dinner," said Austin.

"Maybe breakfast too," Henry said.

"We'll see. I'm sure it'll all work out."

"When will we have the opportunity to visit with you?" Sarah asked, studying Noah.

"Best time is middle of the day. I believe our schedule is full the rest of the time. Check the information in your room and we can set up times to meet," said Noah. "It's your vacation. Enjoy all the activities and get off the boat as often as you can. I understand the onshore excursions are fantastic."

"Are you going to be able to do them, as well?" Sarah asked.

"Like I said, we'll have to check the schedule. I know there's a snorkeling adventure I'd like to try."

"And shopping adventures," said Tara, focusing her attention on Starr.

"That sounds like fun," Starr said, feeling as if she was finding a new friend. She hoped so. This Christmas caper was just beginning, and she might need one. Servers came around with trays of drinks. Noah took two and handed her one. Starr liked that he always seemed to be aware of her and her needs.

Sarah gave him an approving smile. "So, Noah tells us that he met you online. I must tell you that I'm surprised but very pleased to meet you."

"What dating app was it?" Tara asked and waited as if to test Starr.

"Forever Yours," said Starr smoothly, relieved she and Noah had already discussed it. What other questions would come her way?

CHAPTER EIGHT
NOAH

Noah watched Starr react to his family and wondered what it would be like to present a real girlfriend to them. So far, Starr was charming all three adults. The twins were hanging onto her, and she didn't seem to mind.

Rob came over to him. "Looks like this time, you've got a winner. I don't think Mom is going to be pushing Cynthia on you. She was really unhappy when Cynthia told her at the last minute she couldn't come on this trip."

Noah faced away from the women. "Mom doesn't get it, and I won't tell her that Cynthia is dating someone else. It's not my news to share, especially when her parents find out."

Rob clapped a hand on Noah's back. "Well, it doesn't matter now. Mom will have the wedding planned by the time we leave the boat. Guaranteed."

Noah's stomach sank. This charade might backfire on him. But looking at his mother's happy expression, he told himself it might be worth it to give her an enjoyable Christmas.

Tara was quizzing Starr on her job as a first-grade teacher, searching for answers about putting the boys in kindergarten a little early. Noah didn't hear Starr's answer because his mother grabbed his arm and pulled him away from the others.

"I'm annoyed I didn't know about Starr before this, but I'm thrilled you've chosen such a lovely woman to date. I'm thinking you ought to bring her to Boston to celebrate New Year's Eve."

Noah shook his head. "That isn't going to happen. I've already promised an important client that I will be at his party in Miami. I can't and won't disappoint him."

"Well, how about Valentine's Day? Bring Starr to Boston then, and I'll put on a party to introduce her to my friends."

"Whoa! Slow down! We've just started dating. Anything could happen between now and then." His throat had gone dry at the thought of this scheme blowing up in his face.

"What do you mean? You aren't just using her, are you?" His mother asked, demanding an answer with that "don't lie to me" look she'd always used with him.

He shuffled his feet. "I have no intention of hurting her or anyone else. Give us time to see if this is right."

His mother studied him and then nodded. "Okay. But I like Starr. I don't know what's going on with Cynthia, but I'm ready to cross her off my list of hopefuls."

"List of hopefuls? What's that all about?"

It was his mother's turn to look sheepish. "I just try to keep in mind women I think might be a match for you. That's all."

"Stop!" Noah gave his mother a steady look. "I'm a grown man and can handle my life myself. I'll find someone in time. The business has been keeping me busy."

"Not too much for Chip," countered his mother, though her tone had softened considerably. "Don't worry. I only think of ways to help you because I love you so much."

"Love you, too, Mom, but relax. Okay?"

She nodded. "But I will take the time to get to know Starr as much as I can."

"Remember, she's a working member of the cruise staff until after Christmas."

"Yes, I'll take care with that." His mother gave him a quick squeeze and went back to where Tara and Starr were talking.

Noah watched his mother go, wishing he'd never thought of doing this deception. By now, he was sure Starr was regretting it too.

###

After spending another hour with his family while fellow passengers lingered on the deck watching the ship cut through the rolling waves, it was time for Noah to leave to get dressed for his dinner appearances both in the restaurants aboard ship and in the dining room where families with children were sure to congregate. He would be lying if he said he wasn't nervous. Starr was used to dealing with a lot of kids. He wasn't.

"Guess I'd better go," Noah said to his family.

"Where are you going?" asked Austin.

"It's business. Nothing for you to worry about. You'll see me tomorrow." Noah said to him and exchanged smiles with Tara. He hoped the boys wouldn't realize he was playing Santa.

"Do you have time to stay?" Sarah asked Starr.

Starr gave him a beseeching look.

He put his arm around her. "She's going to help me. We'll see you later."

As they walked away, Starr quietly said, "Thank you. I don't want to be left alone with them. I'm exhausted trying not to give anything away."

"You'd better fill me in as I change into costume. And help me cover my hair and face. I don't want Austin and Henry to recognize me."

"No problem." She was silent and then said, "You have a nice family. I'll try to help you as much as possible to keep Austin and Henry from discovering you're Santa. Going forward, Vianna and I will be accompanying you to the dinner visits. But tonight, you're on your own because we've worked all day greeting guests."

"Thanks. Enjoy some time off. After I'm through, which should be about nine thirty or so, will you join me and my family on the Lido deck?"

"Yes. It'll seem odd to your family if I don't. I can always escape early because I have breakfast duty."

"Fair enough." He turned to her. "I really appreciate what you're doing to help me out."

"It's too late to back out now," Starr said. "I hope you come up with a fair excuse about why our relationship didn't work out."

"Yeah, I've thought of it and will have to make it believable. My family really likes you."

They walked into the costume changing room, and after he changed into his Santa costume, Starr made sure his pillowy stomach was in place. Then she fixed his hair and his beard, taking care to cover his dark hair and the whiskers that were shadowing his cheeks.

When they were done, Starr stood back and gave him a look of satisfaction. "Okay, Santa. You're ready."

"I wish you were coming with me," said Noah, hoping he didn't sound too needy. They were just kids who'd be glad to see him, right?

CHAPTER NINE
STARR

Starr left Noah taking off for the dining areas and went to the employee cafeteria. She wanted to get a healthy meal inside her before going to her cabin and resting. The strain of being careful about what she said and how it might affect their caper was emotionally draining. She wanted to tell his family the truth, but she'd promised to help Noah and she would. Still, she vowed never to do something like this again.

She entered the cafeteria, fixed her tray, and smiled at a few people she'd met earlier. But instead of sitting down with them, she chose to sit at a small, single table, needing time to herself.

After completing her meal, she headed to her stateroom hoping to lie down.

She opened her door and stepped back. "What are you doing?

Half-dressed, Vianna looked up from her bed where she was lying with a man Starr didn't know. "What do you think we're doing?"

The man scrambled to his feet. "Sorry. Thought we'd be alone. I'm Nate, a guitar player with the country music band."

"I'll leave now," Starr said tersely.

"No, that isn't right," Nate said. He turned to Vianna. "If you want to hook up later, come to my stateroom." He pulled up his pants, slipped on his cowboy boots, and gave them a little wave as he left the cabin.

"Thanks," grumped Vianna. "He's a really nice guy. Not as rich as I want but nice just the same."

"Look, what you do is your own business. I don't want to

be involved in any way whatsoever. I just need to know that if I want to rest in my cabin, I can."

"I understand. I don't want my uncle to find out about this. Promise?"

Starr nodded. "Promise."

Vianna smiled. "Okay, then. I'll go meet Nate at his cabin." She took a few minutes to freshen up and then left, carelessly closing the door with force.

Starr sat on her bed and sighed. This dream cruise was becoming a nightmare.

Starr went to the passenger's dining hall to see if Santa Claus was there. Noah was walking through the area waving at the kids. He held up a sign that said Santa will be available to talk with kids and have his picture taken with them tomorrow afternoon. Starr stood along the wall, watching as Noah stopped to talk to a child and then move on to speak to another. One rambunctious little boy, who was probably six or seven, got up from his seat and socked Noah in the stomach. Even though he was well-cushioned, and it wouldn't have hurt, Noah couldn't hide his surprise. He knelt beside the boy, looked him in the eye, and quietly talked to him. Before he was through, the boy was crying and accepting a hug from Noah.

Impressed, Starr caught Noah's gaze and gave him a thumbs-up.

"Ho, ho, ho," he said as he waved goodbye and exited the area.

Starr followed him to the costume room, making sure no kids saw them and slipped inside the room with him.

"How'd it go? You were great in the dining room," she said to him.

"Did you see that kid punch me in the stomach? What's wrong with him? Everyone loves Santa Claus, don't they?" Noah shook his head.

"Kids today have it tough in a way I never did not that many years ago. He was obviously acting out, but you handled the situation well. How did you do at the restaurants?"

"That went a little better because the kids didn't have the space to run around. Their parents were right there, and that helped. But I don't know how the store mall Santas do it. They couldn't pay me enough."

"Did Henry and Austin guess who you were?"

"Rob did a great job of diverting any close attention to me. I hope I can make it through a visiting session without them finding out. After I get out of this costume and get washed up, I'll be ready for a drink. Will you join me and my family?"

Starr saw the hopeful look on his face and smiled. "Sure. After all, I'm your girlfriend."

Noah gave her a sheepish grin. "Sorry about that. But it's too late now to change what we've set up. I'll make it up to you somehow."

"Let's just enjoy ourselves tonight and not worry about it," she said, her emotions mixed. There were times when she wished they really were together. He was a very nice man and those tingles she'd felt earlier when his leg touched hers indicated chemistry between them could be very exciting if they ever gave it a try.

Starr waited for Noah to get ready, anxious to celebrate her first night on a cruise ship. With any luck, being with his family wouldn't be a problem.

The Lido deck was crowded with partygoers. At the far end, a huge TV screen showed a band playing as their music blared from loudspeakers, adding hype to the party scene. In front of the screen there was room for dancing, and several people were moving to the beat with abandon. Tables lined the rails of the ship intermittently, allowing space for those who wanted to stand.

Noah led her to where Rob and Tara were sitting.

They smiled at them and waved them to the two empty seats at the table.

"Glad you could make it. Mom is with the kids to give Tara and me some time alone." He waved a waiter over to them. "What'll you have?"

"I'll have a pilsner." said Noah and turned to Starr. "What would you like?"

She thought a glass of red wine might be just what she needed to feel part of the celebration and ordered pinot noir. She gazed out at the dark water delighted to see a streak of golden moonlight cross atop the waves toward her.

"Beautiful, huh?" said Tara. "It seems like forever since Rob and I had a vacation, and this couldn't be better." She smiled at Starr. "Especially with such happy news for Noah. He dated one woman we didn't like, and then there's the issue of Cynthia. She isn't right for him. Everyone but Sarah and Cynthia's mother thinks so. He's been shutting himself off so he won't have to deal with any drama. It's fantastic that you've met. Where did you go on your first date?"

Starr's pulse sprinted inside her. She turned to Noah. "Tara wants to know about our first date. You go ahead and tell the story."

Noah's eyes widened, but he quickly covered it with a smile. "That night in New York?"

She nodded. He'd started this whole thing; he could handle it.

"Remember the time I had a business meeting in New York

before Thanksgiving? That's when it happened."

"After meeting online, right?" prompted Tara.

Noah nodded. "Yes. I know you're interested, but this is all very new and special. When I want to share, I'll let you know." He turned to Starr.

She nodded. "We're trying not to rush things and want to keep as much as possible to ourselves. I hope that doesn't sound rude."

"No, not at all. It's very sweet." She smiled at Noah. "I think this is the first time you've made sense when it comes to choosing someone special."

Relieved the moment had passed, Starr exchanged glances with Noah.

Rob stood and held out his hand to Tara. "Care to dance, Mrs. Jordan?"

Giggling, Tara stood, accepted Rob's hand, and hurried to the dance floor.

Starr turned to Noah. "You didn't handle Tara's question well. I don't think your mom will be happy with your not wanting to share. We need to have a story."

"Yes. Like you, I don't like lying, but I needed to come up with something to keep my over-anxious family at bay. So far, it's working."

"Okay. As long as no one gets hurt, I'll go along with it. I didn't think the family would be so anxious for you to settle down."

"In our twenties, Chip and I raised some hell. But now that we're older and running a business together, things have changed. I guess you could say we've grown up."

"And he's about to get married," said Starr.

"Right," said Noah and took a sip of his beer ending their conversation.

Starr gazed out at the water, becoming entranced by the

scene in front of her. Though she was quiet, her mind was busy. What had started as a lark was rapidly changing for her. It was clear that for Noah, this caper was an excuse for some privacy that would dissolve at the end of the cruise. She knew it was best that way. She had too many life decisions ahead of her to have them become more complicated than they were. One thing she had to change was living in the same town with her ex and his family. A family she once thought she'd have with him.

"Do you want to dance?" Noah asked her.

She shook her head. "No, thanks. In fact, I'm tired. I think I'll go to my cabin."

"Want me to walk you down there?" he asked, sounding concerned as he got to his feet.

"No, thanks. Stay and enjoy your family." She stood as Rob and Tara returned to the table.

"Nice to see you again," Starr said. "I have to get up early to do a breakfast run as an elf. I'll see you tomorrow."

She started to walk away.

"Whoa! Stop! I know you're private about the new relationship but come on. Where's your goodnight kiss?" asked Tara.

Noah glanced at Starr, a question in his expression.

Starr stepped forward and Noah wrapped his arms around her.

" 'Night, Starr," he murmured before he placed his lips on hers.

A bolt of sensation jolted her body. Starr clung to him for a moment and then stepped back, her cheeks on fire.

"Good night," she managed and walked away to sort out her feelings.

CHAPTER TEN
NOAH

Noah watched Starr walk away surprised by the feelings she'd aroused inside him. When she'd reacted to his kiss, his entire body had demanded more. He hadn't felt that way in a long time.

"I really like Starr," said Tara when Noah returned to their table and sat down. "She seems very genuine."

"She is," Noah said and realized how much he'd asked of her. Somehow, he'd make it up to her.

The next morning, a day at sea, he was eating in the staff cafeteria when Vianna walked in. She came right over to him. "How's it going?" she asked.

"Okay. Last night being Santa was a bit of a challenge, but I think today will be better. You and Starr are going to be with me when I have visiting hours with Santa this afternoon. Right?"

Vianna made a face. "You don't really need me there as long as you've got Starr to help, do you?"

"Yes, I do. We need one elf to handle the kids in line and another to help with photographs. What's your problem?"

"I've met someone, and I need to be able to spend time with him."

"He's not going anywhere. We're in the middle of the ocean. He'll have to understand that until Christmas, you've got a job to do."

"Oh, but I don't want him to think I need the money," said Vianna.

Noah shrugged. "I can't help you. And you'd better be there this afternoon to help Santa. Weren't you supposed to be busy greeting kids at breakfast?"

Vianna waved away his concern. "Starr is taking care of it. She's so good with the kids. I'm not."

"I see," Noah said, hating the idea that like he, Vianna was taking advantage of Starr's easy-going nature.

As soon as he finished breakfast, Noah went to find Starr to make sure she was all right on her own. He knew from his experience last night how important that second person was to handle excited kids at breakfast time.

Noah found her surrounded by children in the cafeteria. When she saw him, she gave him a smile but he could see Starr needed some help.

He walked over and started talking to two little boys who looked like brothers. That gave Starr enough space to kneel beside a little girl with brown braids who looked about five.

"What's your name?" Starr asked her as the boys ran away.

"My name is Melody. I'm here with PopPop. Granny is gone."

"Where's PopPop?" Starr asked her after giving Noah a worried look. The little girl was still wearing a nightgown and nothing on her feet.

"He's sick," Melody said. She took hold of Starr's hand. "Come with me."

Starr glanced at Noah.

"I'll come too," he said.

"Thanks," Starr answered. "I'm not sure what to think."

"What cabin are you in?" asked Noah.

Melody stopped and, frowning, clapped a hand to her mouth. Then her face brightened. "I know. D-3-3-4. PopPop practiced with me."

Noah let out a sigh of relief, undecided if they should go to staff or wait until they saw the situation for themselves.

Starr led the way to the elevators, and they took it to D deck and to stateroom 334. The door was slightly ajar, enough to see that they could get inside.

Noah held up his hand. "Let me check first." He walked inside and found an older man in pajamas stretched out on top of one of the twin beds.

He went over to him. "Sir, are you alright?"

The man groaned and sat up. "Will you hand me a juice box from the fridge? I'm a diabetic and need some sugar."

Starr and Melody entered the cabin. "PopPop! I got help." She ran over to him and hugged him.

He hugged her back and accepted the carton of orange juice Noah handed him. "Melody, you did a great job of getting help. It's just how we practiced." He gave Noah and Starr a helpless look. "I'm usually more careful than I was last night, but all the excitement of our cruise has messed me up a bit. I'm Jonathan Kingman, and this is my granddaughter, Melody."

"You're traveling together?" Starr asked him.

"Yes. My wife died a year ago. We'd planned on doing a cruise just before she became ill. I decided to do this in her memory. Melody is with me because she's suffered from the loss of her grandmother and is now dealing with a new baby brother. Her parents and I agreed it would do us both good to be away for a bit."

Now that the man was sitting in a chair, Noah thought he recognized him.

"Where are you from? Boston?" asked Noah.

Jonathan grinned. "Outside of Boston, in suburb called Wellesley. Why?"

"No reason except I'm from the Boston area too and thought I recognized the accent. And if I'm not mistaken, you've recently released a book."

"Guilty as charged," Jonathan answered. "A novel in memory of my wife."

"PopPop, can we go swimming?" Melody asked, climbing into his lap.

He hugged her and set her on her feet. "I don't see why not. Give me a few minutes and we'll get ready."

"My family is aboard the ship and I have two nephews about Melody's age. I'm sure they wouldn't mind if you joined their group."

Jonathan's face lit up. "Why, that would be nice. I'm sure Melody would enjoy the companionship."

Starr gave Noah an approving look. "I'm sure the boys would like it too."

"Here's my phone number. When you're ready, come to the pool deck, and I'll introduce you. My nephews are twins."

"Twins?" said Melody, smiling.

"Yes, I think you can have fun together." Noah laughed as Melody clapped her hands.

Her grandfather gave him a grateful smile. "Thank you. That's very thoughtful of you."

"Perhaps, I'll see you later. Now, I'd better get back to the other kids," said Starr.

Noah accompanied her out of the room, and they stood a moment.

"That was such a nice thing to do," Starr said to him.

"I think it'll work out for everyone. My mother is a huge fan of Jonathan Kingman. She's going to be thrilled."

Starr grinned. "Maybe that will keep the pressure off of us."

"Let's hope so," said Noah, giving her a wink.

CHAPTER ELEVEN
STARR

Later, after Starr changed out of her costume, she went to her stateroom and put on the bikini she'd brought with her. With her fair coloring, she couldn't be in the sun for too long, but she was eager to get to the pool to see what was happening with Noah's family.

It didn't take her long to locate them on the pool deck. While Jonathan and the others watched, Melody played in the pool with Austin and Henry.

Noah noticed her walking toward them and got up from his chair to greet her.

"We saved a chair for you. I think I may have done my family the biggest favor ever by offering to have Jonathan and Melody join us. My mother is thrilled to spend time with him. They've been talking books, the kids are having fun together, and everyone is happy and occupied, which makes it easier for us."

Starr laughed. "Good job." She followed him over to an empty lounge chair next to Tara's.

"'Morning," Tara said cheerfully. "I guess it's almost afternoon. Come relax."

"I can't be in the sun for too long, but I want to get some time in the pool."

"I see you've got suntan lotion." Tara waved Noah over. "Be a gentleman and help put suntan lotion on Starr's back. We can't have her get burned."

Noah and Starr exchanged looks of surprise and then he said, "Sure."

Starr handed Noah the tube of lotion, sat on the empty

chair, and turned her back to him, noticing a smug smile cross Tara's face. It sometimes felt as if Tara was testing them.

As Noah's hands smoothed the lotion on the skin of her back and neck, Starr lowered her face. Tingling nerves brought a hot flush to her cheeks and she was glad no one would be able to tell if it was a reaction to him or being in the sun. But *she* knew. The caress of his fingers on her back made her imagine what it might be like to make love with him.

"Looks like you're doing fine," said Tara before going back to her book.

"Thanks," said Starr and stood. "How's the water?"

Noah's hair was wet. "It's really nice. But why don't we go to the adult pool so we can really swim? The others can watch the kids here."

"Okay," she said. She was beginning to think this whole charade was all wrong. She was attracted to him but couldn't show it. And he wasn't showing any real interest in her.

Starr and Noah sat on the edge of the pool next to one another.

"Thanks for playing along with me," said Noah. "I want this cruise to be a wonderful one for my family. Everyone is getting along, and so far, it's been the best time together we've had since my father died. Mom is almost giddy about talking with Jonathan, and he looks very pleased."

"What's going to happen at the end of the cruise? How are they going to feel then about the two of us?" Starr asked him.

He made a face. "We'll have to deal with it then. I'll think of something. Like you, I don't want anyone to get hurt." He put his arm around her. "You're the best. Let's try to enjoy ourselves."

"Okay," she said. Getting into the water might cool her

attraction to him. Anything was better than sitting beside him with his arm around her. She slid into the water and let out a gasp of pleasure as the coolness caressed her. She flipped on her stomach, found a clear lane, and began to swim. She'd gone a couple of laps when Noah caught up to her and then swam by.

She stopped swimming and grinned when she realized he was trying to impress her.

Noah was standing at the end of the pool waiting for her as she swam up to him. "Showing off, are we?" she said.

He laughed. "I used to swim for my school team. This felt great. And by the way, you're an excellent swimmer. Where'd you learn?"

"At the local Y," she said. "It was a great way to let off steam as I was growing up. I used to be teased about my size and my red hair. Now, it isn't so bad. I've grown taller and my hair is no worse than that of women who dye their hair pink, purple, or blue."

"Ah, I bet the boys loved you," he said. "You're not one of those fussy women who are so worried about getting her hair mussed up that she can't do much of anything."

"I was a bit of a tomboy," she admitted, pleased that he wasn't one of the successful men who wanted their significant other to look polished all the time.

"What are you doing this afternoon?" he asked.

"At two o'clock Vianna and I have to help with the cookie decorating party. Apparently, the ship has a whole bunch of plain sugar cookies that the kids can ice and decorate. It should be a fun mess. When do you have your first Santa talk?"

"This afternoon. And then tonight, I'm to help with the singalong of Christmas carols to take place in the theater at seven. The cruise director has done a great job of planning a lot of cool stuff for the kids."

"She keeps coming up with ideas on how to use us. I found out about the Christmas carol thing just before I came to the pool."

"The nice thing is that after Christmas morning, we'll be on our own." Noah smiled at her. "It'll be great to be able to relax."

"But your family might want us to spend more time with them. We'd better think of different things we've done together. I think Tara suspects something's off between us."

"Yeah, I think you're right. Let's say that one night we went to the theater. Have you seen any plays in New York?"

She shook her head. "Not recently. We'd better think of something else."

"Okay, we can pretend we did touristy things like go to the top of the Empire State Building. I haven't done that in years, but all the information will be online."

"We went to FAO Schwartz and you bought me a fuzzy brown bear."

He laughed. "Okay. I'll go along with that. One of my favorite childhood toys was a bear named Teddy. We'll have to come up with some ideas for dinners we ate. What are your favorite foods?"

"I like Asian food of any kind as well as old-fashioned steak and potatoes."

"Okay, we'll meet in my stateroom and go over some menus online and choose a couple of restaurants that were our favorite. My family knows you haven't been to my apartment. But maybe we should tell them about yours. You'd better describe it to me."

They sat on the edge of the pool, chatting. Starr kicked her feet gently in the water, absorbed in their conversation. When she felt a hand on her shoulder, she jumped.

Tara laughed. "Whoa! You jumped as if you were doing something illegal."

Starr laughed to cover up the shock she'd felt. She and Noah weren't breaking the law, but it sometimes felt that way to her.

"I just wanted to tell you that we've all had enough of the pool and are leaving for lunch and then naps. There's some kind of decorating party for kids at two and I don't want the boys to miss it. Will you take them, Noah? Rob and I just want some time alone."

"I'll be at the party. I'll help Noah keep an eye on them."

"You two are the best together. Cynthia would never have agreed to it." Tara gave them a little wave and walked away.

Starr turned to Noah. "We have enough time for lunch and a planning session before I have to get ready for the party. Let's go. I don't want anything to go wrong."

"And then at three, I'll be talking to the kids and you'll help the photographer, right?" he said.

She nodded. Everything seemed to be happening all at once. But in a few days it would be over.

CHAPTER TWELVE
NOAH

Noah and Starr headed to the employee's cafeteria. It, like the dining hall for the paying passengers, was open most of the day and evening. Starr was right, he thought, to learn more about one another so they could handle questions from his family. Especially Tara.

While Starr picked out a salad, Noah opted for a ham and Swiss cheese sandwich and a coke.

Sitting at a table together, Noah realized how comfortable he was with her. There was not a lot of small talk but a peaceful quiet between them. They ate quickly, and then Noah said, "Let's go to my cabin and make a plan."

As he unlocked the door, he turned to her and grinned. "If things were different between us, this could be a whole lot of fun. But we'll just talk."

Starr gave him a steady look. "Yes."

Inside the cabin, Starr sat in the one chair while Noah stretched out on the bed.

"Let's start with that magical weekend in New York," she said. "I don't often get to the city, so this will be new to me too."

"Okay, my actual meeting was on a Friday. I'd decided to stay in the city for the weekend to meet up with an old pal of mine, a guy I went to prep school with. But instead, I'll say I met you."

"And we went to dinner where?"

"A Thai restaurant on 9th Street. I've been to one there that specializes in Northern Thai food. They have the best duck dish I've ever had. It's a crispy leg with a tamarind sauce."

"Okay, and that evening, what did I have?"

Noah thought a minute. "I know. You had a chicken and lemongrass dish with a curry sauce of some kind."

"Wow! I didn't know you were a foodie," said Starr, giving him a look of approval.

He shrugged. "I've always enjoyed different kinds of food."

"What was I wearing? That's important," said Starr.

"It is? I have no idea. You'll have to come up with that stuff."

"Let's see. How about a little black dress. I've brought one with me for later. You can see it then when we're through with our jobs. Then the next day we do some touristy things."

"Liked we talked about, right?"

"Yes. The Empire State Building, the toy store and whatever else you want to say. That night we ate at an Italian restaurant."

Noah nodded with satisfaction. "There's an excellent one not far from the Empire State Building. We'll say we went there. Then, on Sunday afternoon, we parted ways but kept in touch."

"What about Thanksgiving?" she asked. "We didn't get together then."

"We'll say we were thinking it over because we lived in two different places."

"Perfect. And when I heard about your Santa Claus job, I got the job as an elf so we could spend more time together," said Starr.

"And now, we're trying to see if this will work," Noah said. "And after we get off the ship, I can tell my family that we decided that with me living in Boston, and your refusing to leave Ellenton made it impossible."

Starr frowned. "But, in truth, I'm thinking about leaving Ellenton to get away from my past there with my ex."

Noah saw she was sincere and let out a troubled breath. The situation was becoming all too real.

Starr checked her watch. "I've got to get ready for the icing party."

Noah got up and walked her to the door. As he opened it, Vianna strolled by, stopped, and turned around.

Narrowing her eyes at them, she said, "As long as you don't say a thing about me, I won't mention this. Fair?"

Starr sighed. "I have no intention of getting involved with your activities. And for the record, nothing happened in here. Noah and I were just talking. That's all."

Vianna laughed. "As if I'm going to believe that."

Thinning her lips, Starr waved goodbye to her and left Noah at the door wondering what might've happened between them if he hadn't come up with the plan to fool his family.

CHAPTER THIRTEEN
STARR

Starr looked at the kids surrounding the long table and smiled. Julia had set it up with different colored icing in bowls spread along the length of it. Interspersed were plain sugar cookies shaped into trees and stars, along with un-iced gingerbread men and women. But it was the excitement on the faces of the children that gave her pleasure. She thought of her own first-graders and was surprised by how much she missed them. Before she'd broken up with her ex, she'd been thinking of having children of her own.

Most of the kids had at least one parent with them. She caught sight of Melody and went over to her. "Need help finding a spot?"

Melody smiled at her. "Austin and Henry are saving one for me."

Austin ran up to them. "My uncle has a place for you. C'mon!"

At the end of the table, Noah waved to her, and Starr waved back thinking how lucky he was to have such a congenial family. She loved her own, but being the youngest by nine years had meant there was no real closeness between them. Margaret was two years older than her brother, Michael, and actually nine years older than her. Noah and Rob were much closer, and Tara fit right in with them.

A little girl with dark curls all over her head tugged on Starr's hand, bringing her back to the present. "Can you help me?" the little girl, who looked to be about four, asked.

"Sure. Let's see what cookies you want to decorate, and then you can choose colors. What's your name?"

The girl shuffled her feet, looked down, and then up at her with a shy smile. "Lorena."

Starr watched as Lorena carefully selected three cookies. Two stars and one tree. "Great. Now let's choose some colors for them."

When the girl picked out pink, blue, and yellow, Starr smiled, wondering what color the tree would be. One of the joys of working with kids this age is they weren't restricted by "rules" of proper colors but would be open to seeing things differently.

A boy of about eight came to their side and worked eagerly to spread some icing on top of the two gingerbread men he'd picked out. She observed him make them alike with smiling faces and eyes made with cinnamon candies. He iced blue pants and white shirts for each and then shook multi-colored candy sprinkles all over them.

"Nice job!" she said to him, and Lorena, who'd also been watching, declared she wanted sprinkles too.

Starr chuckled. After eating a lot of this sugar, these kids would need a lot of activity before their bedtime.

A steady flow of children arrived and left. By the time Starr was through helping Julia's staff, she was ready to relax for a while before helping Noah with Santa visits. Then she and Vianna were required to be part of the sing-along tonight, passing out sheets of paper with words of the Christmas Carols on them and doing whatever else Julia asked of them. Tomorrow, they'd dock in George Town, capital of the Cayman Islands. She couldn't wait to see the sights and hoped to buy a new bikini. Later, she'd be busy helping Noah sit with the kids before bedtime. So far, the job hadn't been as bad as she'd once thought it might be.

She went to her cabin, changed into her bathing suit, and headed to the pool deck for a few minutes of sun before going for a swim in the adult pool, which she'd found relaxing.

She found an empty chair and was just settling in it when Tara appeared. "What are you doing here alone? Come sit with us."

"I didn't know if you and Rob wanted some time to yourselves," Starr responded, getting to her feet.

Tara placed a hand on Starr's shoulder and gave her a sweet smile. "Sweetie, you're family. Of course, we want to spend time with you. The boys are taking a rest period after over-indulging with cookies and all the holiday activities. It was a great idea to ice cookies, but it'll make the kids super active and super cranky if they don't get some rest in between activities. Sarah is happy to rest with them. She and Jonathan are having dinner together, while Melody spends time with us. Sweet, huh?"

Starr smiled. "Yes, it is. They sure seemed happy talking together."

"Sarah can be difficult about wanting things to be done properly, but she's a very nice person. Over time, she's learned I'll run my house my way. But she's been lonely, and it's been wonderful that she and Jonathan have struck up a friendship."

"Hi, Starr," said Rob as they approached him. "Where's Noah? He said he'd join us, but he hasn't shown up."

"He's scheduled for Santa visits this afternoon. Maybe he's getting ready."

"Here he is now," said Tara, waving to him across the pool.

He saw them and trotted over through the throngs of filled lounge chairs.

"You all done cleaning up from the cookies?" Noah asked her.

She nodded and smiled. "It was a real mess, but the kids seemed thrilled. They got to carry a small box back to the cabin with them."

"Where are Austin and Henry?" Noah asked Tara.

"In the stateroom with your mother, hopefully getting some rest. She'll bring them to the pool before she gets ready to go to dinner with Jonathan."

"Mom and Jonathan? Really?" Noah asked, and a smile spread across his face.

"This cruise is turning out to be a great thing for her. The best Christmas in a long time," said Rob.

Starr exchanged a quick glance at Noah and let out a soft sigh. They'd have to make it a soft landing for her when Sarah learned things might not be what she thought.

"C'mon, bro! I'll race you in the water," said Rob.

They headed off together, leaving Tara and Starr alone.

"You and Noah seem so compatible," said Tara. "Now, can you tell me about your first date?"

"You mean the visit in New York? Sure," said Starr, relieved she and Noah had planned it out. She quickly recited what she and Noah had talked about. "I don't get to New York that often even though I live upstate."

"I can't get over the fact that Noah has kept quiet about this … this relationship. But then, neither he nor Rob are especially chatty. It's a guy thing, I guess. I was hoping for a daughter of my own. If your relationship with Noah continues and you end up married to him, I hope you'll be willing to let me spoil any little girls you might have."

"Whoa!" Starr stiffened and held up her hand to ward off any such suggestions. "We're in no position to even think of a future. We really are just getting to know one another. I live in Upstate New York, and he lives in Boston. That's just one of the reasons we can't plan far ahead."

"Okay, I get it. Sorry. I hope I didn't upset you too much. I tend to be overly enthusiastic about things."

"Thanks. I'm glad you understand," said Starr sincerely.

She'd laid the groundwork for a possible reason she and Noah wouldn't work out. The thought troubled her, but she couldn't think about it. Just a few days more and she'd be free to go her own way.

The men came back, grabbed towels, and sat down on chairs beside them.

"How's the water?" Starr asked.

"Great," said Noah. "The pool is heated."

"What's everyone planning to do in George Town tomorrow?" asked Tara. "Rob is going horseback riding on the beach with the boys. I want to have lunch and do some shopping."

"I've signed up for a boat tour with snorkeling," said Noah.

The three of them turned to Starr.

"I thought I'd look around the town, visit shops on Cardinal Avenue," said Starr.

"Let's do it together," said Tara.

"Okay. That'll be fun," Starr said. "There's also a National Museum we might want to see." She loved to learn about new places.

"Hi, Mom!" came a chorus of voices, and they turned as Austin and Henry ran up to them with Sarah behind. "Can we go swimming now?"

"Sure. C'mon. I'll go in with you." Tara stood. "See you later, Starr. I'm so glad we'll get to spend some time together tomorrow."

After the rest of the family joined Tara and the boys in the pool, Noah turned to her. "Guess you and Tara are getting along nicely."

"Yes, I've already mentioned the difficulty of a lasting relationship between you and me with the two of us living in different places."

"Great," said Noah, giving her a smile before lifting his face to the sun and closing his eyes.

"Time to get ready for Santa visits," Starr said.

Noah scrambled to his feet. "I'd almost forgotten about it. Good thing you're here to remind me."

They walked to their cabins together.

CHAPTER FOURTEEN
NOAH

Later, dressed in the Santa costume, Noah made his way through the dining hall, stopping to shake a white-gloved hand with kids and parents. He liked how great he felt when the faces of the people he met, no matter the age, lit with excitement at seeing him. He tried to ignore how his sunburned skin itched beneath his costume and went to the atrium for Santa Claus visits.

When he arrived, a decorated chair, more like a throne, was waiting for him, along with Starr and Vianna as elves and a woman who was the ship's photographer. In front of his seat was a long line of children. He drew in a deep breath and told himself he could do this.

Starr walked over to him. "Ready?"

"As ready as I'll ever be. Help me with that kid who likes to punch me in the stomach. And don't let Austin and Henry come sit or stand by me together. It'll be trouble for sure."

"Okay. Not much longer, then we'll be free to be ourselves," Starr said.

When he realized how short the cruise and their time together was, he felt a frown forming.

The photographer approached. "First, let me get a picture of you, Santa, sitting in the chair, with an elf on either side of you. We'll use that in promo material going forward."

She took the photo and then Vianna waved the first child in line to come forward.

As he met with each child, Noah was caught up in conversations wrapped around memories of his own childhood. While the toys of today were all electronic, there was still a hopeful tone to the children's requests that touched him, and he realized how fortunate he'd been.

He looked up to find Austin and Henry facing him.

Starr went over to them.

The two boys stared at Starr with wide eyes.

"I know you," said Austin. "You're Uncle Noah's girlfriend!"

"You know Santa Claus?" Henry said, awestruck.

"Does Uncle Noah know you work for Santa?" Austin asked.

"He might not like it," said Henry. "He doesn't have a lot of girlfriends."

Noah held in his laughter and watched as Starr tried to get control of the conversation.

"I'm sure your Uncle Noah would approve of a job like mine," said Starr "Now, who wants to go first? Just one person at a time."

"I will," said Austin, glancing at his brother.

Henry nodded.

"Ho, ho, ho!" said Noah to Austin, leaning away from him. "And what do you wish for this Christmas?"

"I wish Uncle Noah would marry Starr," Austin said clearly. "She's an elf."

Noah coughed to hide his laughter, then said, "And why should she marry Uncle Noah?"

"Because it will make my grandmother happy, and Dad said it's been a while since she's been so happy."

"I see," said Noah. "And what do you wish for yourself?"

"That's easy. I want an iPad like my friend, Brady."

"We'll see if Santa has that for you. Merry Christmas!"

As Austin walked away, Noah shook his head. He was certain Rob and Tara were behind Austin's request. He gazed at Starr and seeing how her cheeks had grown a bright pink, he knew she'd heard the exchange.

Henry ran up to him. "Hi, Santa. Do you know my Uncle Noah? His girlfriend is right there." He pointed to Starr.

Noah nodded. "Yes, I ... I know everyone. What do you want for Christmas?"

"I want an iPad like my brother and Brady. Thank you very much."

Henry turned to walk away, stopped, and stared at Starr, before giving her a little wave as an impish smile crossed his face. Then he ran to catch up to Austin who was standing with Rob. The smile Rob gave Noah was as impish as his son's.

Noah shook his head. His family was ... well, persistent.

It was so late by the time Noah was through with Santa visits that he didn't bother to change out of his costume for the dinner he grabbed in the employee cafeteria. He was due to make rounds in the restaurants before the singalong.

Starr ate with him and then announced she was going to rest before heading to the theater.

Alone in the cafeteria, Noah thought about this crazy experience and knew it was something he'd never forget.

Later, when he stepped inside the Italian restaurant on his rounds, he saw his mother and Jonathan smiling and talking at a table. He went to the other tables with children and then quietly moved on his way. Seeing his mother flirt with a man made him uncomfortable, but he liked how happy she seemed. For all his success, Jonathan was a down-to-earth, pleasant man who obviously loved his granddaughter and seemed to be enjoying his growing friendship with Noah's mother.

After Noah had made the rounds of the four restaurants, he returned to the cafeteria and greeted people there before going to the auditorium where the sing-along was to take place. When he got there, one of the singers running the program waved him over.

"Can you sing? One of our guys is sick and we could use your help leading the singing in one of the back sections of the theater."

Noah nodded. "I can help you out." There was no way he was going to tell him he was teased for being in the seventh-grade glee club. It had been a difficult time in his life before he realized it was cool to be a geek who was a whiz at IT information and a baseball player who could pitch.

Starr and Vianna appeared in costume and as directed, they stood at the door as people entered the theater and handed out sheets of paper with the lyrics of the carols.

Standing in front with the other three singers, Noah couldn't keep his eyes off Starr. She was very cute talking to the kids. Like Tara, she'd make a good mother one day. Startled by his thoughts, Noah concentrated on the piano music that began, even as the room was filling fast with passengers.

After the crowd was settled in their seats, the piano player rose and announced that he'd begin playing the music for the carols in the same order as printed on the sheets of paper handed out. He smiled at Noah. "And tonight, we have Santa and his elves with us. When you leave the room, be sure to pick up your special Christmas ornament from one of the elves to take to your room as a souvenir of this night. And remember, Christmas Eve, Santa will be receiving visitors in the afternoon. If you haven't signed up for a spot, be sure to do so. He and the elves will stay as late as they must to take care of everyone."

The music began, and Noah headed to the back section to help the singers. He exchanged a smile with Starr who happened to be on his side of the theater and began to sing the first carol. His voice rang out loud and true.

From the corner of his eye, he saw Starr give him a thumbs up. He grinned and sang even louder.

Later, in the changing room, Noah, Starr, and Vianna got out of their costumes.

"What a night," grumbled Vianna. "I thought those carols would never end."

"Wait until tomorrow. It might be our last day in costume but it's going to be a long one," said Starr. "Santa will receive children before dinner."

"Yeah," agreed Noah. "And later, we have to help deliver presents to the staterooms."

"Seriously? That's Julia's job," said Vianna.

"We're all expected to help her. Most of the cabins and staterooms have requested them," said Noah. "C'mon. It hasn't been that bad. We have one more day, and then we'll be free."

"This gig hasn't kept the two of you from being together," said Vianna. "I still want to find someone for me. It's a long story, but I really need to do this."

"I get it." Noah looked at Starr. She glanced at him and looked away.

He reminded himself that he'd be part of their charade for only a few days more.

CHAPTER FIFTEEN
STARR

Clutching her small purse to her, Starr sat in a tender with a number of other passengers from *Tropical Promise* for the fifteen-minute ride to the George Town dock. No passenger would be allowed to enter Grand Cayman without his or her passport. Having never been out of the country, Starr was thrilled by the idea.

After passing through customs, Starr went through the gates and waited on Harbor Drive for Tara to meet her.

Soon, Starr saw Rob, Tara, and the boys, followed by Noah and his mother. She waved and walked over to them.

"Hi," said Noah. "I'm going to go snorkeling and will catch up with you later, back on the ship."

"Have fun," she said, and noticing the rest of the family staring at them wasn't surprised when Noah gave her an almost apologetic look and then kissed her on the cheek.

"You two definitely need some time alone together," said Tara, shaking her head.

Starr's cheeks flamed with heat, but she remained quiet.

"The boys and I will see you later. We're going to find where we meet the horses for our beach ride," said Rob.

Tara kissed each of them and turned to Starr and Sarah. "Okay, girls, we're free to go shopping. I've heard about all kinds of bargains here. We can start with the Bayshore Mall. I was told we can walk there from here at the South Terminal."

"I believe the Cayman Islands National Museum is close by," said Starr. "I don't know if anyone else is interested."

Sarah smiled. "I'm going to meet Jonathan there in a while. But I'll stay with you two until he's free. Melody is staying with the boys after they all take a beach ride."

Tara reached over and clasped Sarah's hand. "I'm happy you've found someone to do things with on our cruise."

"Thank you, dear," Sarah said. "It's been very nice for me. He's such an interesting man."

"One thing I want to do is have a mudslide. It's the drink of the Cayman Islands and is supposed to be delicious. And it's safe because I'm not driving," said Tara.

"A schoolteacher friend told me about mudslides," said Starr. "I'm going to try it, but she warned me to have only one. Besides, I'm not much of a drinker."

"What are you hoping to buy?" Tara asked her.

"A new bathing suit."

"Your bikini looks great on you," said Tara. "I used to have a great figure before having twins and staying at home."

Sarah placed a hand on Tara's shoulder. "You're fine, Tara. Beautiful."

Starr listened to the exchange with interest. Sarah might be insistent on Noah finding someone soon, but she obviously already had a sweet relationship with Tara. That was important to anyone joining the family.

They walked along Harbor Drive and easily found the massive Bayshore Mall.

"Well, we ought to be able to find something here," said Sarah.

"And they have food and a bar, too," said Tara. "I don't know about anyone else, but it's going to be fun for me to wander around without any little ones to keep an eye on."

Starr walked into and out of the shops telling herself not to succumb to temptation. It felt like a wonderland of opportunity to buy lots of things at low prices. But she was saving her money for a Mexican silver bracelet in Cozumel. What she did need was a new bathing suit. And, okay, a T-shirt or two. That's all.

The warm air, the white sandy beach, turquoise water, and bright blue sky wrapped her in satisfaction. Back home, it was a typical time of cold with rain or snow.

After a while, Sarah left them to meet Jonathan.

Tara suggested getting some lunch, and in looking around, they found a restaurant that advertised Chicken Goan Curry with a Caribbean touch.

Tara turned to her with a smile. "Are you game?"

Starr grinned. "I love curry dishes."

They went inside and were seated at a table in the shade on the open deck.

"Tell me about Goan curry dishes," Starr said to their waiter.

"It's special. A delicate, mellow flavor-balancing sweet coconut and warm spices with floral lime leaves and tangy tamarind." He gave her a bright, white smile. "You'll like it."

"Okay, sold," Starr said. "I'll do the Chicken Goan."

"Me, too, and then I want to try a mudslide. I think I'd better have food first." Tara smiled at him.

He nodded. "Wise choices."

Tara turned to Starr with a grin that lit her eyes. "I can't believe we're here. It was so unexpected. But sometimes last-minute changes work out well. I'm glad you're here with us. I'm not entirely convinced that everything you and Noah are telling us is the absolute truth, but I'll go along with it because I can see the way you look at one another. And I can't tell you how thrilled the boys are about their Uncle Noah dating an elf."

Starr laughed with Tara and tried to ignore the way her nerves were reacting to the talk of dating Noah. She'd listened carefully to Noah talk kindly to the children, encouraging them to speak up. If she hadn't already thought herself in love with him, she would've fallen for him for certain then. But she couldn't let anyone know.

"It's all very sudden, like we've said," she told Tara. "Now show me your new ring."

Tara held out her right hand. On her fourth finger she wore a ring in white gold with a cushion-shaped, dark Tanzanite and an aquamarine stone on either side. The combination of the rich violet blue with the soft aquamarine was stunning and would, Starr was sure, always be a reminder of the colors around them on this trip.

"Rob is going to be surprised but pleased. He told me to get something nice for myself for Christmas, and I love it."

"It's gorgeous," said Starr.

"We've been looking for a special ring for me for our last anniversary, and this is perfect," said Tara, studying her hand, gazing at the stones. "Now, how about showing me your swim suit."

Starr lifted a bright lime-green bikini from her plastic bag. "I decided to go bright. Do you like it?"

Tara grinned. "I love it. On you, it's going to look great. It seems on this shopping trip, we've both had success."

The waiter brought their meals to them, and they dug in.

"This is so delicious," said Starr, storing all the sensations in her mind to share with her teacher friends later.

After they finished their meal, the waiter brought them their mudslides. "Okay, what is it?" Starr asked before taking a sip.

"Vodka, Kahlua, and Bailey's Irish cream. Pretty simple," he said.

"Pretty lethal," said Tara. "Good thing we're walking."

He laughed. "You'll be fine."

Tara lifted her glass. "Here's to us. I hope things happen so we can be friends for a long time."

Starr clicked her glass against Tara's. She couldn't think of the right thing to say, so she just smiled.

They were still sitting and talking when Tara got a message on her cell. She looked at it "Rob and the kids are back from their ride on the beach and are finishing lunch at a restaurant not far from here. He wants me to meet him and help him take the kids to the turtle farm here on the island."

"Go! While you do that, I'm going to visit the museum," said Starr, excited for the chance to do that.

After they finished up at the restaurant, they parted ways, and Starr walked over to the museum.

She'd read that the museum was in the former Old Courts Building and was dedicated to the preservation, research, and display of all aspects of Caymanian heritage. Prisoners once called this building the "Old Gaol" when it served as a jail and courthouse. Today, the local phrase "walking the 12 steps" meant you were about to have an unpleasant appointment with the judge.

Starr arrived at the two-story white building eager to see the art and artifacts inside.

After she paid a small fee, she saw there were several free exhibits – A natural history gallery, a cultural history gallery, a collection of artworks and others including a visit to the Old Gaol, or jail. She loved the bright blue walls of the art collection, which offset the bright, vivid colors of most of the works of art. She reveled in the idea of experiencing something entirely new to her. Guessing it was part of her love of learning and teaching, she spent an hour there.

She didn't see Sarah and Jonathan and realized they were probably at lunch somewhere.

Satisfied with her time, Starr headed back to the dock for a return trip to the ship.

CHAPTER SIXTEEN
NOAH

Noah was sunburned, tired, and happy when he boarded the ship once more in time for afternoon Santa visits. The snorkeling trip was something he'd always remember, especially swimming with the stingrays. Seeing them glide along the sandy floor of the water like shadows while he swam nearby was a thrill. It was worth all the times he'd had to dress in costume for kids who were constantly tugging at him.

He went directly to his cabin to shower and get ready for his afternoon and nightly duties. If he had time, he could take a quick nap. The sun and salt water had taken a toll on him.

Later, he rolled over on top of his bed to check the time and scrambled to a sitting position. He had just enough time to get changed and started on his afternoon visits before his nightly rounds and late-night gift distributions.

He hurried to the wardrobe room and quickly changed into his costume. Starr and Vianna's costumes were already gone, which meant they'd already started. This afternoon, they were handing out little gift bags to kids who wanted them. Julia had informed them that the little gifts and games inside were in lieu of candy canes and other sweets.

He hurried into the atrium and over to his seat. A number of kids were already in line, but after the initial crush, he figured it wouldn't take too long to speak to each one.

Starr and Vianna were a help, keeping the kids in line, talking to them as they became restless waiting their turn. After a busy day off the ship, a lot of them were worn out.

It was almost five o'clock when he stepped into the dining

hall. After a day of shore excursions for most families, the place was packed. Starr waved to him and continued to reach into a decorated box for bags to hand out. He went right over to her. "Hi, before we get together with my family later this evening, we have to talk."

She gave him a questioning look and nodded.

Noah went back to his place by the door and then began circulating through the room in a pattern he'd developed so as not to miss anyone. Starr and Vianna waited by the door for him to finish, and then the three of them headed for the restaurants before going back to the dining hall and starting the process over again, meeting with new kids.

As he worked the rooms in a jovial manner, his stomach growled. His nap had prevented him from eating before he began the stint as Santa Claus.

By nine o'clock, the three of them were done and headed to the costume changing room.

"Almost done," said Vianna. "If after tonight I never see this costume, it'll be much too soon. What are you two doing now?"

"Starr and I are going to join my family," said Noah, cutting off any reply Starr might have made. She frowned but nodded at the seriousness on his face.

"Okay, I'll see you later," said Vianna. "I've met some single people. Guess I'll try to meet up with them."

After she left, Noah turned to Starr. "Sorry to speak for you, but we need to talk. My brother took me aside this morning and told me he didn't know what was going on, but you and I aren't acting like we're a romantic couple. He told me my mother is going to realize that and warned me not to screw up this cruise for her."

"What exactly does he want us to do?" Starr asked.

Noah swallowed his discomfort. "We need to touch each

other, kiss, and act like we really care. As I've promised you, I'll come up with a reason for the breakup after the cruise ends."

Starr wet her lips and wiped her hands on her pants. "Okay. I agree. We can't ruin the holidays for them."

Noah stepped forward, cupped her face in his hands and planted his lips on hers.

As they kissed, Starr's arms came up around his neck and he moved closer to her, his heart beating so fast he was sure she could hear it.

He forced himself to step away and drew a deep breath. "How was that?"

Starr put a hand to her pink cheeks and stared at him wide-eyed. "Excellent."

He put an arm around her and pulled her close. "We'll have to practice more, but I think that was believable." He kissed her on the cheek. "This too."

Starr gazed up at him and nodded.

CHAPTER SEVENTEEN

STARR

S tarr was still reeling from Noah's kisses when she said, "I'm going to my cabin to freshen up before we meet with your family."

"Me, too," said Noah. "Do you want me to escort you to them?"

Starr smiled her gratitude. "That would be great." This whole new dimension to their fake relationship was jarring. She'd have to act as if she liked it when she was supposed to be simply helping him out of an awkward situation. The real trouble was, she truly did like it. She was still tingling from his kisses. She'd thought he was hot, but now that she knew him in a different way, she thought he was even hotter.

A short while later, hand in hand, they walked toward his family. She was relieved to see that Sarah wasn't with Rob and Tara, and she figured she must be with the boys. Before leaving her cabin, she and Noah talked again about the need to throw off Rob and Tara's suspicion that this whole thing was a hoax.

Playing along, Noah threw his arm around her as they stood to talk to them.

"Want to see my new ring?" Tara said, holding out her hand to Noah. "Rob got it for me for Christmas and our anniversary."

"Tara picked it out in town. We've been looking for the right one for a while," explained Rob.

"Starr and I had fun shopping. We even tried out a

mudslide drink," said Tara. She turned to Starr. "You missed out on the turtle farm with the kids. How was the museum?"

Starr smiled. "It was interesting. They suggest it takes about an hour to go through it, so I wasn't there long. But they had plenty of information to share—lots of artifacts. And I love the big, bold colors of some of the paintings I saw." She gazed at Noah. "Of course, I missed being with Noah, but I was glad he could go snorkeling."

Noah smiled at her and gave her an affectionate squeeze. "Has everyone notified the Purser on board that we're getting off the ship tomorrow to go into Cozumel for Christmas Day? He needs to let Customs know."

"Yes," said Rob. "I've taken care of Mom, Tara, and the kids."

Noah turned to Starr.

She smiled and nodded. "Julia reminded me earlier. I can't wait to say I've been to Mexico. I know it may sound lame to you three, but it's a big deal for me."

"It's always fun to travel to different places, and I'm glad we're all going to see Cozumel together," said Tara, and Starr realized how much she liked her.

The four of them sat on stools at one of the outdoor bars and sipped cool, refreshing drinks—beers for the men and margaritas for Tara and her.

Starr wondered what it would be like if she decided to leave Ellenton, maybe move to someplace warm. She loved the idea of being in shorts and a T-shirt year-round.

Tara nudged her. "What are you thinking about? You're smiling."

"Just wondering what it would be like to live in warm weather. This cruise has been so nice," Starr replied.

"I love summer in Boston and on the Cape," said Tara, "but it would be nice to get away to warmth more often during the winter. But Rob and the boys like to ski, so there's that."

"I guess every place has its good points and bad," said Starr. She realized as she spoke that Noah was listening in on their conversation.

"You're thinking of leaving Ellenton?" he said.

"I have a lot to consider," answered Starr, "but I can't do anything until after the school year. My kids need me."

"What do you say to that?" Tara asked Noah.

Starr leaned forward to hear his response.

"Like Starr says, it's a lot to think about. I respect that for her," Noah said and wrapped an arm around her.

She smiled at him, hoping it was the end of the conversation.

Shortly before midnight, Starr joined Julia and her other helpers to begin the distribution of gifts. Families coming on board had the option of sending gifts ahead and having them delivered Christmas Eve or they could sign up for a generic basket of goodies to be delivered. Not everyone signed up, but Julia would need all the help she could get. Thankfully, Julia changed her mind at the last minute and allowed Noah, Vianna, and Starr to wear regular clothes so they could move faster.

Seeing how well organized it was, Starr's admiration for Julia grew. She knew now what being a social director involved and realized it was a huge undertaking on any cruise.

Noah approached her. "This might be the best part of our job. It's going to be fun playing Santa Claus this way. Did you believe in him when you were little?"

Starr smiled and nodded. "Yes and no. My brother and sister played along for years, but when I found out he wasn't exactly real, my mother explained that Santa is the spirit of giving, and that's he's very real year-round."

"Ah, that's really nice," he said. "Rob and I knew before our parents realized we did. But I've always thought Christmas was a magical time."

Each of the helpers was assigned to a deck. Starr was glad she'd be working with Noah. Vianna was working on a different deck with the musician Starr had seen her with and seemed very pleased about it, holding onto his hand and smiling up at him.

Julia had laid out piles of gifts according to deck levels and Starr saw how busy they'd be. Still, it was fun to help other passengers celebrate.

Several foldable garden carts were waiting to be filled with gifts to speed the process.

"Remember people, no talking, laughing, or noise of any kind should be made while you're roaming the hallways," said Julia. "That would ruin everything. Now, go! I want this wrapped up as quickly as possible."

"Let's try to put our packages in room number order," Noah said to her. "That seems like the easiest way to do it."

"Great idea. Are you always so logical?"

He smiled and shrugged. "Pretty much. That's why I'm good at my job."

She laughed. "Okay, smartie, let's do it. Then I'll be ready for bed."

He raised his eyebrows and gave her a roguish look.

She laughed again. "You know what I mean. I want to be ready to go into Cozumel."

But as they went about sorting packages and delivering them, Starr couldn't help wondering what it would be like to make love with him.

They'd just delivered the last package when Noah said, "Want to go up to the Lido deck for a breath of fresh air? I'll even buy you a drink to celebrate the last of Santa and his elves."

"Sounds great. It was more work than I thought. Besides I want to enjoy the peace and quiet and sit in the moonlight. It's something I've always dreamed of doing if I ever had the chance to go on a cruise."

"This job hasn't been bad, but I'm glad we're moving ahead without being scheduled to make appearances in costumes. I must admit, though, that having Santa Claus aboard the ship has made it special for Austin and Henry. I'm relieved they can't do more than suspect I was the one playing Santa. I'll never admit it to them."

Starr laughed. "They're super boys and very active."

They reached the open deck and stood quietly by the rail watching dark waves move in a steady rhythm below them. A golden trail of moonlight crossed the water and Starr thought of the yellow brick road in The Wizard of Oz and felt as if she were in a place as different as it was for Dorothy. She looked up at the canopy of stars sparkling like jewels and wished she could reach up and touch them. The air was cooler than she'd thought, and she couldn't prevent a shiver from crossing her shoulders.

"Cold?" Noah asked and wrapped an arm around her.

She nodded and nestled close to him, then gazed at him.

At sea in his light-blue eyes, she didn't object when his lips met hers and they shared a kiss that filled her with longing.

With her eyes closed, she felt rather than saw his sudden movement away from her.

He shook his head. "I'm sorry. I know we promised one another this was a game only. You've made it clear that sex is out of the picture and if I keep going, that's where it might end up."

Starr swallowed hard and straightened her top. "You're

right. This is a cruise ship caper, nothing serious."

"But we still have to put up a believable front for Rob and Tara and my mother," Noah said, giving her a steady look.

"Yes, I promised you I'd do that, and I keep my word. It's late. I'm going to bed."

"If you don't mind, I'm going to stay here and cool down. See you tomorrow."

"Merry Christmas," she said, with a soft tremor in her voice. She glanced at him, but he'd turned his back to her.

CHAPTER EIGHTEEN
NOAH

L ying in bed alone, Noah felt like a horny teenager. He and Starr had made a deal, and he'd honor it. But damn! He wanted to make love to her. But then, where would that lead him? Nowhere, because he didn't know how they could have a future with him living in Boston and Starr living in New York. He didn't want to hurt her. She brought out very protective feelings in him.

Getting back into the Christmas spirit, he couldn't wait to surprise Starr with a private tour of the Cozumel Mayan ruins and beach. She'd talked about wanting to see as much as she could, and this would be a perfect thank you gift.

Noah awoke to a knocking on his door. Grumbling to himself, he got out of bed wondering why staff would be bothering him at his early hour.

He opened the door to find Rob, Tara, Henry, and Austin smiling at him.

"Merry Christmas!" they cried softly so as not to disturb the other passengers.

The boys barged into the room carrying a package between them.

"Open it up!" cried Austin.

"It's for you," Henry said.

Noah hugged Tara, clapped Rob on the back, and turned to the boys who'd thrown themselves on his bed.

"Here," said Austin. He handed Noah the soft package.

"It's kind of silly, but we wanted you to have something to

open," said Tara.

Noah took the wrapping off and stared at the T-shirt with the Christmas Cruise colorful graphic and grinned. It would be the perfect way to remember this crazy time.

"Great! Thanks," he said, accepting hugs from both boys. "Merry Christmas! Did Santa come to you?"

Austin and Henry grinned at one another and said in a chorus, "iPads!"

"Great! Santa knew just what you wanted, even when you weren't at home. I like it."

"Me, too," said Tara. "Santa magically did his job."

He exchanged secret smiles with her and knew he wanted a family like Rob's.

After they left, Noah took a shower and got dressed, anxious to give Starr her gift.

Noah knocked softly on Starr's cabin door, hoping she was awake. He heard noises and waited for her or Vianna to respond.

Moments later, Starr, fully dressed, stepped outside into the hallway. "Merry Christmas. You're up early."

"Rob, Tara, and the boys stopped off with my Christmas gift." He brushed the front of the T-shirt he was wearing and grinned. "Nice, huh?"

"Very nice," she said.

"I have a gift for you," Noah said. "I've arranged for us to go on a private tour of Cozumel's Mayan ruins and beach. I know you like to learn about places you're visiting and thought you might like this."

She looked up at him with shiny eyes. "That's so thoughtful of you. Thanks so much! I'm sorry, but I don't have a present for you."

"You have given me the best present on this cruise by playing your part. I signed up for the morning session figuring you'd want to do shopping afterwards," Noah said. "Is that okay?"

"Okay? It's perfect."

At her smile, he filled with pleasure.

They walked up to the staff cafeteria together. Though they didn't have any duties, they were still considered hired crew.

The lines were busy, but they were able to get breakfast quickly and sit down to eat.

"Vianna must have stayed over in the musician's cabin because she never showed up in the one we shared."

"I have a feeling that relationship won't last beyond the cruise," said Noah. He'd never liked Vianna's flirting. She seemed like a desperate woman.

"Cruise relationships usually don't last," said Starr matter-of-factly, and Noah realized her statement bothered him. He knew they were only friends who'd vowed to remain that way, but he really liked Starr. A lot.

They ate quietly for a while; then Starr said, "I'm going up to the Lido deck and look around. They'll let us know when we can line up to get off the boat. I think it's supposed to be around nine o'clock."

"Okay, I'm going to go see my mother. I'll meet you in line then. Be sure to bring a bathing suit in case you want to go swimming. The jeep I've hired will meet us at the dock."

Satisfied with a filling breakfast of bacon and eggs and a freshly baked muffin, Noah headed for his mother's stateroom to wish her a Merry Christmas. This idea of shaking up their normal routines was turning into a superb one.

His mother answered the door dressed for the day. "Hello, Noah. Merry Christmas! What a wonderful way to celebrate the holiday here on the ship."

"Yes, it's a beautiful day out there." They hugged, and he handed her a small package. "It's the best I could do here."

She smiled and ruffled his hair. "Just having my family on a trip like this is enough for me." She opened the box and read the note he'd placed inside. Chuckling, she said, "I'm going to hold you to this. A dinner at the restaurant of my choice? I can already think of a couple of places I'd love to try. Thanks so much. I have something for you at home."

He laughed. "I promise to come and visit you. What have you got planned for the day?"

"Jonathan and I, Rob and Tara, and the kids are going to do some snorkeling. Rob found a place that has snorkeling aboard a glass-bottom boat which means the kids can see the marine life below them and where the adults are snorkeling. The boys, I know, will be happy just to be in the boat or swimming in shallow water."

"Sounds great. I've arranged for Starr and me to take a tour to see the Mayan ruins and the beach. Should be a fun excursion."

His mother gave him a steady look. "Just what is going on between the two of you? I can't decide if you're merely interested, or falling in love."

Noah blinked in shock. "What? We are just getting to know one another."

"Well, in case you want my opinion, Starr's a very nice woman and I really like her."

"That's good to know," Noah said stiffly, glad he and Starr wouldn't be spending the day with his family. It was getting too difficult.

CHAPTER NINETEEN
STARR

S tarr sent a text message wishing a Merry Christmas to her parents and to her siblings. She could well imagine them in their homes celebrating and was glad that she, her parents' only single child, wouldn't be sitting with them thinking of Reggie's betrayal. She'd been right to get out of town for the holidays. Until now, she hadn't thought of her heartbreak over Reggie.

She leaned against the rail of the ship and gazed out at the beautiful turquoise water. Feeling the warm air on her body, she was thrilled to spend the holiday like this. And, she admitted to herself, with Noah. He'd mentioned he didn't like aggressive women like Vianna, and she was too afraid of her feelings for him to voice them aloud.

Checking her watch, Starr decided to head down to her cabin to get some sneakers and her fanny pack. She wanted to be able to take some photos and to hike comfortably.

When she returned to the open deck to get in line for disembarking, she saw Noah already there. He waved her over and handed her a brochure.

She studied the photo of the ruins and read that San Gervasio is an archaeological site of the Pre-Columbian Maya civilization.

"It's located in the northern third of the island off the northeastern coast of the Yucatan Peninsula," said Noah. "I've been reading this. I think we're going to like it."

"Thanks so much," said Starr. "It's a wonderful gift."

They got off the ship and met their driver, a jovial young man called Alejandro. He drove a turquoise Jeep with a removable top that remained in place.

"We can take off the top, if you wish," he said in impeccable English with a bit of a British accent. "But I leave it on for those who wish to stay out of the sun."

Starr raised her hand. "That would be me. I burn very easily." She put on the straw hat she'd bought on the ship.

He smiled and nodded, tapping his tan baseball hat with a logo that read Mayan Tour Company.

"Okay, I think we're ready. I have plenty of cold water with me and snacks. And when we get to the beach, I have towels for you, and bug spray if we need it."

"Wow, you've thought of everything," said Starr.

"I'm the number one tour guide on the island," said Alejandro proudly.

Starr and Noah exchanged smiles and climbed into the jeep.

As Alejandro drove, he spoke into a microphone so they could easily hear him.

"Once we arrive at the archaeological site, we'll make our way down a small nature path to get to the ruins. San Gervasio was a significant site for Mayan women who would travel there to pay homage to the goddess of birth and fertility. There are a total of nine temples."

"Interesting," said Starr.

Alejandro continued. "Though this site isn't as popular as Chichén Itzá, it's famous in its own right and should, I believe, be seen. It dates back to 100 BC and extends to the 16th century."

"Pretty impressive," said Noah.

"It will take approximately a half-hour to get there, so feel free to relax and enjoy the scenery," said Alejandro. "I'm here to answer any questions you might have. In the meantime, I'll play some music for you."

Relieved to have some quiet time, Starr gazed out at the turquoise water and lush greenery and wanted to pinch herself to make sure she wasn't living in a dream.

Noah seemed to sense what she was thinking and reached over and gave her hand a squeeze.

She squeezed back and leaned against the seat and closed her eyes lulled by the guitar music playing in the background. It was all so different from her usual holidays.

Later, looking at the abandoned structures, Starr marveled at the site.

Alejandro stood between Noah and her and explained, "The temples were built from hand-cut limestone blocks. The temples themselves usually contained one or more rooms, the rooms so narrow they could only have been used on ceremonial occasions not meant for the public."

"What about other features?" Noah asked.

"Temples were often pyramids with steep stone stairs leading to the summit, where significant ceremonial rituals and sacrifices were performed. Some of their religious ceremonies included human sacrifice."

"And Mayans sacrificed animals to appease gods for a variety of reasons. Right?" said Noah.

Alejandro nodded. "Though many, like jaguars, deer, turtles, spider monkeys and various birds, were commonly revered. It's interesting to read about the Mayan history and culture. You might want to pick up a book about it."

Walking around the structures, Starr was struck by how ancient people must have struggled to survive. The temples were impressive with their size and purposes. But when she looked at them, she saw the hard work and care that must have gone into making them.

Noah came up to her and put his arm around her. "Almost intimidating, huh."

"Exactly."

"How about a swim? Did you bring a suit?"

"I'm wearing one beneath my sundress, and a swim sounds lovely." She held onto his arm bringing him to a stop so she could face him. "Thank you for bringing me here. It's something I'll always remember."

His gaze met hers and he smiled. "Me, too."

"Next stop is Stingray Beach. It has all kinds of facilities there, and you can even swim with the stingrays. Sound okay?" asked Alejandro.

"Oh, yes," said Starr delighted. She hadn't gone snorkeling yet, and this would be a great opportunity.

Alejandro drove them into the park and said, "I'll wait for you. Stay as long as you wish. I've kept my time open." He handed them each a beach towel. "If you wish, I can keep all your valuables with me."

"Thanks," said Noah. "I'll take care of any overtime and extras."

Onsite, there was a snack bar along with a shower area and dressing rooms. The whole park was geared to tourism, and Starr felt comfortable there.

"Let's swim now, and we can have lunch later. Does that sound okay to you? Noah asked her. He took off his shirt and shorts and handed them to Alejandro.

"It sounds perfect." She slid out of her dress, handed it to Alejandro and stood a moment gazing around her. She looked out at the water and observed caged areas where they kept the stingrays and nurse sharks they advertised.

"I looked up information on Stingray Beach before I

booked the tour," said Noah. "They say they're the only place that performs work and activities for the restoration and conservation of corals through the introduction of Artificial Marine Habitats and the relocation of hard coral colonies from the seabed to habitats."

"That's impressive," said Starr. "I like to hear that."

"You'll like this too. One of their activities is to free up to 60% of their captive-born animals in order to support the growth of the stingray population. Pretty great, huh?"

"Very," Starr quickly agreed.

They signed up to swim with the stingrays. Because Starr hadn't snorkeled before, she opted to stay in shallow water without the need to rent gear. She'd already signed up for the snorkeling tour in Nassau and wanted also to be able to spend time shopping.

Later, standing in the water, Starr learned how to touch stingrays by always using the flat of her hands and stroking it down the center of its back. Just as she'd been told, the skin of the creature was soft and supple.

She glanced at Noah. His face held a look of wonder as he touched one.

"Stingrays are curious and playful animals," explained Luis, the guide who was helping them. "They will engage in playful behavior just for their amusement. But if they feel threatened, their first instinct is to swim away. Still, you must respect their space."

"They're really cool," said Noah. "This one likes us."

"Keep feeding it squid and it'll hang around," said their guide. "Most rays will wait for your gentle touch in exchange for the food in your hand. And, Starr, it's considered good luck for seven years if you kiss a stingray on its head. Try it. We'll take a photo of it."

"Go ahead. I want to see that," said Noah.

Starr gazed at the stingray, swallowed hard, and gave it a quick kiss before handing it squid. Later, seeing the photograph of herself, Starr laughed for the pure joy of it. This trip was so much fun.

"Here's a photo of the two of us," said Noah, handing her a second photo he'd bought.

Starr studied the two of them and her heart ached. They looked so happy together.

CHAPTER TWENTY
NOAH

Noah waited for Starr when she entered another jewelry store specializing in silver. She was determined to buy a bracelet in Mexico. While she was looking, he made a quick trip back to one of the stores where he'd seen something for her as a farewell gift.

He felt the package in his pocket and let out a troubled sigh. He was having so much fun with Starr it was sometimes hard to remember this was all part of a plan to fool his family, nothing real.

When she finally emerged from the store, Starr went over to him and lifted her arm to show him her purchase. Her bracelet was smooth and round, and it fit her dainty wrist perfectly. Its simplicity was so much prettier than some of the fancier ones they'd looked at together.

"Okay, I'm ready to go back to the ship," Starr said. "Are you?"

"I was ready a while ago," he said. "I'm going to take a swim in the pool and grab a cool drink."

"That sounds perfect. I might even take a nap. It's going to be a lazy day at sea tomorrow and the next day we'll hit Nassau."

"Wow! The time is going fast," he said as they walked back to the ship. So far, the trip had exceeded all his expectations.

After they boarded the ship, Noah didn't see Starr until she joined his family on the Lido deck after dinner. It had felt strange to be by himself and he realized he'd become accustomed to being with her.

"Hi, Starr," said Tara. "I heard you kissed a stingray. What was that like?"

"Better than some of the men I've dated," she quipped, and everyone laughed.

Noah held up his hands in self-defense. "She's not talking about me."

As the laughter increased, Noah wrapped an arm around Starr and squeezed.

Still laughing, she looked up at him with green eyes filled with mischief.

His heart stuttered and then picked up speed.

They sat at a table and exchanged events of the day. Henry and Austin, tired from the sun and the day's activities, sat in their parents' laps.

"Are you still an elf?" Henry asked. "You're not wearing the right clothes."

"My time helping Santa is over," said Starr. "He's gone back to the North Pole and doesn't need me anymore."

"Will you be with Santa next year?" asked Austin.

Starr glanced at Noah and said, "We'll see."

Noah could tell the boys' remarks made Starr uncomfortable, but he was pleased she was spending this time with his family.

"Tomorrow, I've reserved a private room at the Italian restaurant for all of us, plus Jonathan and Melody," his mother announced. "The staff is being extra nice about it because tomorrow, while we're at sea, Jonathan is giving a little talk about his latest book."

"Great," said Noah, "because Starr and I have been eating in the staff cafeteria, and that will be so much better."

"Yes, thank you for including me," Starr said.

"My dear, I hope to include you in many family plans going

forward," Sarah said, giving her a sweet smile.

Starr sent a warning signal to Noah.

He barely nodded and turned to his mother. "Mom, please stop. Starr and I have just met. We're still exploring our friendship."

"Oh, but, we all love Starr," said his mother.

"I know," Noah said, dreading the end of the cruise and his time with his fake girlfriend.

CHAPTER TWENTY-ONE

STARR

With no job requirements expected of her, Starr awoke late, feeling as if she were on a cruise like everyone else. She looked over at the twin bed next to hers and saw that Vianna was still asleep. Quietly, so as not to disturb her, Starr got dressed in her bikini, put a wrap on over it, grabbed her hat, book, and suntan lotion and headed for the cafeteria.

In line, she opted for a scrambled egg and wheat toast, a cup of coffee, and a sweet roll. For the rest of the day she wouldn't eat much as she waited for the dinner party Noah's mother had set up for the family. Jonathan's talk was at three o'clock, and she planned to listen to his presentation. Other than that, she wanted to sun, swim, and read with no thought other than to enjoy herself. She was happy just sitting by the rail watching the water's movement, well aware she might never get the chance to take another cruise.

Starr left the cafeteria and headed for the Lido deck where she hoped to snag a seat overlooking the water. Taking a seat at a small table, she lifted her face to the sun, loving the feel of the breeze across her face. After a few moments, she pulled her sunhat low to protect her face and opened her book.

Later, she was lost in the story when Noah appeared. "How's your day off?" he asked, giving her a teasing smile.

"Wonderful," she sighed. "How about you? What are you doing today?"

"Like you, I want to hang around, get some sun. Rob and I are going to the casino later, but right now, I've got nothing to do."

"Are you going to hear Jonathan's talk?"

Noah nodded. "I am. The relationship between him and my mother is growing. I think they might be in love, and if that's the case, I'd better get to know him. Funny how it happened so fast."

"You don't think it's just one of those cruise romances?" she asked.

"No. My mother has had plenty of chances to date, but she's never been interested until she met Jonathan. But then, they talk together as if they've always known one another."

"That's sweet," said Starr. "And falling in love can happen quickly."

Noah stared at her.

She swam in his light-blue gaze feeling as if she was drowning. She thought he'd say something, maybe even kiss her, but he simply smiled at her.

"There you two are," said Tara approaching them with the two boys. "We're going to take a swim. Want to join us?"

"Not now," said Starr. "I'm reading my book. If you're still swimming later, I'll join you."

Austin held up a picture book with a turtle on the front of it. "Will you read to me after I swim?"

"I'd like to, but we'll have to see about the timing. You've been learning a lot about turtles, haven't you?"

Austin nodded, and Henry cried, "Me, too!"

She chuckled. The boys were so cute. She glanced at Noah wondering what his children would look like.

He caught her glance and grinned as if he knew what she was thinking.

Starr quickly looked away. The last thing she should be doing is dreaming of such things. As difficult as it was to realize she might never see him after the cruise, a deal was a deal.

###

That evening, Starr took a look at herself in the mirror hoping she'd pass muster. Her cheeks were pink from the sun, highlighting the freckles that were spreading across her nose. The salt air kept her hair in disarray, but her red curls were soft, not bristly. The sleeveless green dress she was wearing looked nice with her lightly tanned skin.

Telling herself she was fine, she turned away. What did it matter anyway?

But when she saw the look of admiration on Noah's face when he picked her up, she knew all her fussing was worth it. Besides, this was her one glamorous evening aboard the ship.

"You look ... beautiful," Noah said.

"Thank you," she responded, her pulse racing.

He took her by the arm. "Let's go. We don't want to be late."

Starr had seen the Italian restaurant, of course, but as she was seated by a host at the long table in the private dining room, she gained a whole new perspective of how beautiful it really was. Crisp white-linen tablecloths covered the table. Crystal water goblets and wine glasses sat at each place. Silverware sparkled in the candlelight. If she hadn't realized they were at sea, she could believe she was in an upscale restaurant in New York.

Sarah and Jonathan acted as hosts of the evening, and seeing them together, Starr understood what Noah had said about them falling in love. In fact, they acted like a long-married couple.

"It's lovely that the family can all be together," Sarah said. "Especially when Austin and Henry and Melody are part of this." She smiled at the boys, and they straightened at the approving look she gave them, while Melody blew her a kiss and giggled. It was a darling moment.

"I appreciate the support you all gave me at my talk this afternoon. I sold a few books and connected with new fans because of it." Jonathan smiled. "It was great to see your familiar faces."

Sarah raised her glass of wine. "Because we have the little ones with us, we'll go ahead and order dinner. But first, I want to give a toast to all of us. Here's to health and happiness."

"Hear! Hear!" said Jonathan, and the rest of them joined in, Starr included.

From there, menus were passed out, and waiters stood by to take orders.

Sitting beside Noah, Starr studied their choices and quickly chose a crab and avocado bruschetta to start, veal piccata for the main course, and a Caesar salad.

Noah chose prosciutto-wrapped shrimp, a prime, bone-in NY strip steak, and a caprese salad.

As their first-courses were served, Starr thought everything looked delicious and reveled in the opportunity to have an evening like this. Even the children eating their pizza did so with unusual decorum.

Tara, sitting on the other side of her, leaned over and whispered, "I hope you and Noah are able to move forward. It would be so lovely to have you in the family."

Starr gave her a smile and shook her head. "We'll have to see. That's all I can say."

"I'll give Noah a talking to if it doesn't," Tara said.

Starr knew she meant it and held in a sob. What had started as a cruise caper was becoming very complicated. Even now, though she wished it could work out between Noah and her, she knew she could do nothing about it.

###

After dinner, the group went up to the Lido deck.

"We're down to two nights left on this journey," said Sarah. "The time is going too fast. What plans do you have for tomorrow? She asked Starr.

"I've signed up for a snorkeling tour to Rose Island Beach," said Starr. "It's supposed to be very special. I was lucky to get two tickets. Noah bought me my tour yesterday, so I'm buying his tour tomorrow."

"Very nice," said Sarah. "I like your independence. I'm not sure what I'm doing tomorrow."

Jonathan smiled at her. "Whatever it is, we'll do it together."

"Oh, yes," she said. "The children like being together too, so that makes it nice."

"There's a swimming pig's tour I think they'll like," said Jonathan. "I was hoping we could do that."

"Pigs can't fly, but they can swim?" Sarah said laughing. "This I have to see."

Jonathan wrapped an arm around her. "You're so easy to be with. I love it."

She gazed up at him, and they kissed.

Noah looked at Starr and drew her closer. "It's been a great evening, huh?"

She looked up at him, and he lowered his lips to hers for a quick kiss.

"Why's everyone kissing?" Austin said.

"Because it's a nice thing to do," said Rob. "Wait until you get older. You'll like it, too."

Tara and Jonathan left soon after with the kids to get them changed into bathing suits for an evening swim.

"Anything to tire them out," said Rob, and Starr laughed with the others. The children had been well behaved at dinner, but they needed to get out some of their energy.

"I think I'm going to turn in early," Starr announced. "I have to be up early to go on the snorkeling tour tomorrow. Thank you, Sarah, for a lovely dinner. It was delicious and so fun to be with you all."

"I'll walk you down to your room," said Noah.

"Of course," said Sarah. "As a gentleman, you should."

Starr smiled at Noah, knowing there was no way she could refuse.

They headed down to the lower deck together.

When they got to the door of her cabin, she turned to him. "I don't want to keep you from going back to your family. Thanks for seeing me 'home'."

He laughed and bent forward and kissed her.

She couldn't hold back a sigh and happily went into his arms.

"For God's sake, get a room. And not mine," Vianna growled as she approached.

Noah and Starr jumped apart and gazed at one another.

"'Night," Starr said, both disappointed and relieved that the kiss hadn't escalated into something more. How could she take a chance like that when Noah had made it clear their so called "relationship" would be over at the end of the cruise.

CHAPTER TWENTY-TWO
NOAH

Noah walked away from Starr knowing if he was alone on the cruise and without an obligation to his family, he'd ask Starr to come back to his room. But their agreement, the difference in where they lived, and the fact that they hardly knew each other made it such an illogical choice he couldn't ignore it.

But, later, up on deck with his family, he felt the space beside him empty. Damn! He had to be careful with Starr. It was a relationship going nowhere.

He stared out at the moving waves made darker by the moon hidden by clouds. Gazing at the eerie look of them, he sensed a warning.

Shortly afterward, he bid goodnight and turned in for a restless night.

CHAPTER TWENTY-THREE
STARR

Starr awoke and rubbed her eyes. Weird dreams had kept her tossing and turning. Thinking about them, she realized some of her restlessness was because of her unfulfilled feelings for Noah. That was something she could do nothing about.

Her thoughts turned to the day ahead. Sad it was her last full day on the ship, she was nevertheless thrilled with the idea of the shore excursion to Rose Island for snorkeling. It was a delightful way to end the cruise. She was especially glad she'd have this time with Noah. It would make an excellent memory for her to treasure during the next few cold months in Ellenton.

She put on her new bikini, shorts and a top, washed her face, combed her hair, and headed to the cafeteria. Suntan lotion would come later.

Standing in line, she caught a glance of Noah sitting with one of the female performers and studied him for a moment. He was laughing at something the woman said and he looked ... well, adorable. He wore shorts and a T-shirt that showed off his fit body, and she wondered what it would feel like to go to bed with him. Flustered, she almost spilled the tray of food she was carrying to an empty table.

Noah caught sight of her and waved her over. "Hi, Starr. Have you met Jillian? She's one of the singers in the jazz group on board."

"Hello," said Starr. "I haven't seen you perform yet, but I heard your group was great."

"Thanks." Jillian got to her feet. "Why don't you sit here?

I'm about to leave." She turned to Noah. "If we ever get to Boston to perform, I'll definitely look you up." She held up a business card. "Thanks."

Starr sat in Jillian's empty seat. "What was that all about?"

"Jillian knows a friend of mine, a schoolmate, and she's hoping that after she leaves her tour of cruise ships, her group can get something established on land, so to speak. I told her that Boston had a thriving jazz scene."

"I haven't spent much time there, but everyone tells me it's an exciting city."

"It is. Great restaurants, interesting culture, terrific sailing in the summer, lots going on. I really like it." Noah sipped his coffee while she ate.

When she was through, Noah stood. "Are you ready to disembark in Nassau?"

"Almost. I've got my passport, a towel, suntan lotion, and a hat to take with me on the motorboat ride. Are you set?"

Noah nodded. "Thanks for this tour. I'm excited that we snorkel near a reef and then get to snorkel in turtle-filled water. I haven't done this before."

"I'm thrilled to end our trip this way. From the three day excursions, I will have learned a lot and done some things I've never experienced."

"It was a fluke for me to be on the cruise as Santa Claus, but I'm glad I did it. Let's make this last day count." Noah lifted a hand for a high-five, and Starr slapped it.

Later, aboard the motorboat, Starr watched the changing colors of the water as the sun shone and then hid behind a big, puffy white cloud. The light turquoise shade was her favorite color. The water beneath the boat was so clear she could see into its depths.

"We're passing by Paradise Island on our way to Rose Island Beach and will travel by other islands and beautiful villas, so keep an eye out for them," the captain announced.

Starr couldn't imagine living in such beauty year-round.

"We'll hang out on the beach snorkeling and relaxing at Rose Island as well as visit a coral reef just off the island," continued Justice. "You'll be able to see colorful fish and even a turtle or two."

Starr observed the grin on Noah's face and couldn't help the smile that spread across her own.

Later, on the beach, Starr was fit with fins, a mask, and her breathing tube. Because she was smaller than some others, she wanted to make sure she was given a snug mask and a mouthpiece that fit her.

Satisfied at last, he said, "I think you're ready. Walk into the water and slip your swim fins on, adjust your mask, and I'll watch while you get used to breathing through the tube. When you're comfortable, you'll be ready to swim off the beach. Later, we'll take you to the coral reef."

Masked up and breathing comfortably, Starr lowered her face in the water delighted to see that even this close to shore fish were swimming nearby.

More comfortable, she went into deeper water following Noah closely. Looking down, she felt as if she'd discovered a whole new world. She'd seen pictures of it, but experiencing it for herself was that much better.

For an instant her eyes watered with gratefulness to think she was so lucky.

A tug from Noah pulled her into the moment and when he pointed, she saw a whole school of bright fish swim by.

Later, sitting on the shore with the other twelve people in

their party, an older woman smiled at Starr and Noah sitting together. "It's lovely to see young couples so happy together."

Not knowing what to say, Starr turned to Noah.

"We're just dating," he said, dismissing more conversation.

The woman gazed at them, and the corners of her lips lifted as if she didn't believe him.

"Is everyone ready to take a look at the coral reef?" asked the captain, and the group got to their feet to board the boat.

In the water, it was hard for Starr to keep her breathing steady when her instinct was to gasp at such beauty. The abundance of fish and other underwater life was breathtaking.

When a huge turtle swam by, Noah went underwater to swim with it. She watched him from the surface, mesmerized by the ease and agility of them both.

And later, riding back to the where they'd joined the group on shore, she was pleased when he held her hand. He seemed to know how much she'd enjoyed sharing this experience with him. She realized she wanted more than a pretend relationship with him. She wanted the real thing.

CHAPTER TWENTY-FOUR
NOAH

Noah knew he was in trouble, but he was helpless to do anything about it. If he tried to make a move on Starr, she knew the chances of making their relationship work were pretty low. She'd mentioned at one point that she couldn't leave her students in Ellenton, and his home was in Boston. It was feeling more and more like a cruise romance that wasn't even real.

Looking at Julia's invitation for the staff party in the staff cafeteria, Noah decided to attend. He had to do as much as possible to keep busy on this last night aboard the ship. Tomorrow morning would arrive in a hurry. In fact, passengers were advised in order to make the morning easier, suitcases and luggage had to be outside cabin doors before midnight. Passengers could then pick up their luggage the next day after going through customs and immigration.

Noah was fine with that. Anything to make it easier to leave the ship and get back to his normal life. A few days in Miami and attending the New Year's Eve party put on by an important client would help shake off the experience of being with Starr. He shook his head. Like that was going to happen.

He went up on deck for a drink before dinner and the party.

Rob was on the Lido deck sitting by the pool watching the boys swim with Melody. When he saw Noah, he waved him over.

"Hey, bro, did you have a good day?"

"The snorkeling was incredible. How about you?"

"I got in some snorkeling while the kids were swimming with pigs. It was all very cool. I'm going to have a hard time getting back into my usual routine. How about you?"

"Yeah, this has been a great trip. I'm staying in Miami until after New Year's Day. But then, back to the grind."

Rob's gaze remained on him. "What about Starr? Tell me what you two are doing about a long-distance relationship? How's that going to work?"

Noah made a face and shrugged unable to face the thought.

"Starr is a keeper. Remember that," said Rob, getting to his feet as Tara approached.

Noah waved at her and moved away quickly, certain he couldn't handle Tara's questions. The idea of not seeing Starr every day in the future was tearing him apart.

Later, drinking, dancing, and playing games with the other crew members, Noah thought the staff party was a great way to end the cruise. Julia had gone out of her way to make it a fun time with plenty of food and drinks and party games that became hilarious as time passed.

At one point, Starr came up to him. "I don't know if I'll see you in the morning with all the commotion. So, I'll say goodbye now. Thanks for making my first cruise so much fun. And keep in touch. I've got your number, and you've got mine."

She stood there, looking uncertain, and then kissed him on the cheek before hurrying away. He was about to go after her, when someone called his name to tell him it was his turn to play in the game. Sighing, he turned back.

CHAPTER TWENTY-FIVE
STARR

The next morning, Starr awoke with a sense of dread that stayed with her as she got a quick breakfast and prepared to disembark.

Noah caught up with her as she was about to leave. "Wait for me outside. Okay?"

She nodded, uncertain if it was better to leave without another goodbye or if she'd be cheating herself out of another memory.

After going through immigration and customs, she waited in the crowd in the area where ground transportation was provided. She hadn't decided on a hotel for her New Year's Eve stay but thought she'd try her luck in Coral Gables.

Noah and his family found her standing there.

Starr observed Noah as he said goodbye to the Jordans and tried to swallow the lump in her throat. The time on the cruise had flown by. She hadn't realized how much she loved Noah's family, especially Tara. In a few short days, she'd felt as if she belonged with them.

Jonathan and Melody bid her a safe journey and stood by as Noah's mother came over to her. "I hope to see you in Boston soon." She put her arms around Starr and gave her a strong hug. They hadn't talked that much, but Sarah's approval meant a lot to her, even if it wouldn't go beyond this moment.

After hugging Noah, Tara came over to her. "I hope whatever this is between you and Noah continues. I've never seen him so happy, so relaxed. You two are meant for one another. I know it."

Too emotional to speak, Starr nodded and then cleared her throat. "Thanks for being so sweet to me. I really appreciate it."

"Like Sarah says, we want to see you in Boston as soon as possible. Have fun in Miami and be in touch with me. You've got my information on your phone."

Rob was holding onto both boys with firm hands but bobbed his head at her.

"Have a safe trip back home," Starr said as she and Tara hugged.

Noah's family left, and Starr stood with Noah and their luggage at the curb.

He stared at her and said, "I'm glad we have this moment together. I almost forgot. I have something for you, something to remember this Christmas cruise." He reached into his pocket and pulled out a box Starr recognized from a store in Cozumel. He handed it to her. "Go ahead and open it."

With shaking hands, she lifted the lid off the box.

Nestled against the cotton lining was a tiny, three-dimensional silver teddy bear on a silver chain.

"It's part of our story. Remember? I bought you a teddy bear at F.A.O. Schwartz in New York."

Tears filled Starr's eyes even as she laughed. "It's beautiful! Please help me put it on."

Noah clasped it around her neck and then stood back. "Thanks for all you did for me. You were a real sport about it."

The tears in her eyes spilled down her cheeks. The magic was over. She reached for her luggage and stepped off the curb.

"Look out!" Noah clutched her arm and pulled her back as a bus whizzed by her, brushing against her body, making her rock on her feet, tossing her suitcase to the ground.

Noah pulled her into his arms and grabbed her suitcase.

"You're okay now, but you have to watch your step in this area."

Starr covered her face and tried to catch the breath that escaped her. "Oh, my God! I almost got run over! You saved my life! Thank you!" Overcome with emotion, she leaned against his chest.

"Listen," Noah said, lifting her face and gazing into her eyes with a worried look. "I know we promised to end our relationship after we got off the ship. But I can't. You told me you wanted to spend New Year's Eve in Miami. Why don't you come with me? I've got a room at the W in South Beach and an invitation from a client for a great party. It'll be fun."

Trying to absorb his words, Starr stared at him dumbly as she felt her body drain of adrenaline.

Noah took hold of her hand. "What do you say? Like I said, it'll be good fun and give us a chance to know one another even better."

"Yes, I'd like that." She hoped staying with him would give her time to sort her feelings before heading back to Ellenton. She couldn't face her family like this—happy and heartbroken.

"Okay, then. C'mon!" Making sure the way was clear, Noah led her across the street to where a line of cabs and Ubers were waiting.

CHAPTER TWENTY-SIX
NOAH

As they made their way to the hotel, Noah held Starr's hand. The image of the bus heading right toward her was burned into his brain. Still shaken, he glanced at her staring out the cab's window and realized he'd gone and done it, fallen in love with Starr. People might say what he felt was typical of a cruise romance, something that would eventually become meaningless. He didn't think so, but maybe being together off the boat would help them both see the truth.

At the hotel he had booked, he was pleased to see his client had assigned him an ocean view suite with an oversized balcony. That would make things easier. If Starr wanted to keep to her space, the couch in the living area looked comfy and cozy enough for either of them.

"It's gorgeous!" Starr cried, clapping her hands, and running to the sliding door in the living area leading to their balcony.

"The balcony extends from the bedroom as well," said the bell boy. He led them to the bedroom where a king size bed, desk and chair, and more living space led to the outdoor balcony. After placing both their suitcases inside the room, he stood by.

"Wow! I could live here," said Starr softly.

Noah and the bellman both laughed, bringing a pink flush to Starr's cheeks.

Pleased they'd have such beautiful accommodations for the next few days, Noah tipped the bellman and closed the door behind him, leaving him alone with Starr.

"Noah! This is beautiful!" gushed Starr throwing her arms around him for an exuberant hug before stepping back.

"It's thanks to my client that we have this room," he said, but he was extraordinarily pleased by her response and became determined to show her a good time.

"Let's enjoy the cheese and crackers, fruit, and other treats with a taste of the wine that he ordered for the room."

"Okay," said Starr, plopping down on the plush white sofa. "I feel decadent and pampered."

He chuckled and then became serious. "Do you want to keep your bags in the master bedroom, or should we find another place for them?" He held his breath.

She turned and studied him, letting her green-eyed gaze rest on him. Then with a decision made, she said, "Let's keep them there."

He smiled at her. "I'd like that." Aboard the ship with his family, he'd felt constricted by them. Here, he hoped to explore his relationship with Starr, see if a future together was real.

He opened the bottle of pinot noir that had been left in the room for them and poured some in each glass.

"Here's to a Happy New Year," he said, smiling at Starr. "And to time spent together."

She lifted her glass, and when her gaze met his, he felt a pull inside him and couldn't wait to show her how attracted he was to her.

They sprawled on the couch in the living room, sipping wine, nibbling on cheese and crackers, and talking.

Starr's voice still held a note of pain when she talked briefly about her ex-boyfriend but then her voice changed, became full of determination. "I know what I want now, and I'm willing to wait until I find it in a relationship. How about you, Noah?"

He swallowed hard and then said, "I have a clear idea about what I want in a mate."

She studied him and nodded.

He pulled her to him. "Right now, let's enjoy one another's company."

She looked up at him. "This is a beautiful spot, a rare vacation time, and I'm here to enjoy it."

"Good," he said, setting down his wine glass and lowering his lips to hers.

Starr shifted, moving closer to him, responding to his kiss, fitting against his body.

Lying down, they held onto one another, extending their kiss.

Noah felt his heart fill in a way he hadn't thought possible as lust mixed with awe and tenderness.

After making love, Starr nestled on the bed beside him, fitting perfectly with his body.

She smiled at him and murmured, "That was wonderful."

"*You* are wonderful," he said. "You have no idea how long I've wanted to make love to you. But we had that agreement, and I didn't want to mess things up."

"What's going to happen to us?" Starr asked.

He brushed a curl away from her cheek. "We'll both have to answer that question. But, for now, let's enjoy our time."

"Okay," she said, leaning forward and placing her lips on his.

CHAPTER TWENTY-SEVEN

STARR

Showered and dressed for a casual night out in a sundress and shawl, Starr waited for Noah to finish a business call in the living room. It was interesting to hear his end of the conversation.

"No, that isn't logical," he said to someone. "Remember, anything goes until it comes to the test of logic. If something doesn't pass muster there, it won't work."

Starr wandered over to the sliding glass door and looked out at the water, palm trees, sand, and pool below. What she was doing with Noah didn't pass the test of logic. Was she fooling herself into thinking something might be able to work out between them?

She sighed and turned away. The best thing for her to do was to simply enjoy the next few days with no promise of a future with Noah. Though she was uneasy, she reminded herself that any relationship begins with a learning phase.

Wanting to put a little more sunscreen on her face, she went back to the bedroom.

A moment later, she heard a knock on their door and waited for Noah to answer it.

"Noah, darling! Your mother told me you were here. I came as quickly as I could after breaking up with Eric. I'm so happy you're staying here. I love Miami Beach. So much shopping."

Starr crept to the doorway and peered out.

A tall, blonde was kissing Noah. Wearing a tight, knit mini dress that showed off long, tanned legs, she clung to him.

"Whoa," said Noah stepping back.

"No, you can't get away from me!" The blonde moved closer

to him. "I'm finally ready to say yes to you. When I heard you had a shipboard romance going on for the Christmas cruise, I realized how much I was missing. You're the perfect husband for me. You know our parents have wanted this forever, and I'm prepared."

"Stop, Cynthia," said Noah, moving her away from him. "I have a guest here. Someone I care about."

Cynthia placed her hands on her hips and glared at him. "Don't tell me it's that woman from the ship. You know it will never last. I hear she's a schoolteacher. You need to have someone from our background to be with you, to support your business."

Starr's heart pounded. How dare that woman belittle teaching? She thought of the sweet little faces who depended on her to help guide them through the process of learning and felt her temper rise. Not wanting to be part of the ongoing scene, she stepped out onto the balcony and shut the door behind her. This was Noah's business. Not hers.

She didn't know how long she stayed there when she heard the slider open behind her.

"Starr, come on in and meet Cynthia Withers, a family friend," said Noah.

Reluctantly, she turned and followed him inside.

The way Cynthia gazed at her simple, bargain sundress made Starr straighten. She refused to be intimated by someone like her.

"Cynthia, this is Starr Snowden. I told her you were a family friend and that's the truth. And in spite of that, I'm asking you to leave. I'm sure there are other places you can stay. Perhaps in your family's condo down the beach?"

Cynthia squeezed her lips together and then forced a smile. "Okay, if that's the way you want to play it, I'll leave. But I won't be so eager to say 'yes' again."

"There won't be a next time," said Noah quietly but firmly. He went to the door and held it open.

With a last look at Starr, she left.

"I'm sorry," said Noah.

"I heard some of it before going out on the deck. She really wants to marry you," Starr said.

"She wants to marry my money," said Noah with a scornful laugh. "C'mon, let's go out and forget her visit ever happened."

"All right," she said, but her growing confidence about being with Noah had been struck a blow.

Later that night, as they lay in bed together, Noah stroked her back. "I don't want you to ever think I'm going to change my mind about Cynthia. It's just a cute family story, this idea of our ever marrying after I announced it in second grade."

"But she said you needed someone with a similar background for your business," Starr said.

"That kind of thing is so outdated as to be laughable. I have a great business partner and we're able to carry on and grow our business without the idea of spouses helping us. We've already proven that."

"But didn't you tell me Chip is recently engaged?"

"Yes, but that doesn't mean I have to be," said Noah, and Starr could tell he was getting irritated by the circumstance.

"We don't have to dwell on it," she said in soothing tones.

Noah turned to her and cupped her face in his broad hands. "You're perfect."

When his lips met hers, she responded, feeling as if she was in the right place. He made her feel coveted.

Aware of the differences between them following Cynthia's visit, Starr decided not to think about when she'd have to fly home. She and Noah had two more days to enjoy the weather and being together. She wouldn't think of anything else because if she did, she'd have to face the fact that being here in South Beach with Noah for New Year's Eve felt an awful lot like being on a cruise with him, that once it ended, their relationship was over.

As if he felt the same way, Noah fussed over her.

After a luxurious breakfast in bed which Noah ordered for her after she'd told him she'd never had one, he suggested they go walking on the beach.

In front of the hotel a walkway trailed beside the beach, making it easy to travel some distance and to see the other beautiful hotels there. Some of the hotels had several cabanas lining the beach in front of them for their guests to enjoy.

"Do you want to go shopping?" Noah asked her that lazy afternoon.

She shook her head. "No, thank you. I've spent a lot of money already." She didn't remark about teachers' salaries being so low, but the truth was many teachers could never afford the vacation she was having. "I would like to spend some time reading."

"Really? That's great. I have some work to do and want to look up something on my computer."

"By all means, go ahead," she said. "We're both on vacation and should do what pleases us."

"You're so different from some of the women I've dated," he said, pulling her close and kissing her.

Time stood still as they spent another night together, giving Starr the illusion that this could last forever. But when she awoke, she realized this was her last full day with Noah. Already she was worried about meeting his client and the people he'd invited to what she could only envision was a gala.

When the time came to get dressed, she pulled out the strapless black dress she'd borrowed from Parker's pre-baby days. Simple and classic, it would do.

CHAPTER TWENTY-EIGHT
NOAH

Knowing how nervous Starr was about meeting his business associates, Noah waited patiently for her to appear. He had plenty to think about as he stepped out onto the balcony of his hotel room.

Feeling the warm, gentle breeze on his cheeks, he remembered how Starr's hands had caressed him during their lovemaking and knew their relationship couldn't end. He wouldn't let it.

"Okay, I'm as ready as I'll ever be," said Starr behind him.

He turned and felt his heart stop before gathering speed. She looked ... well, stunning. Dressed in a short black, strapless dress and high strappy sandals, she smiled at him. Her red hair was a mass of soft curls that looked like a halo around her face. He stared at the silver teddy bear necklace she'd chosen to wear, and knew he was right about her.

"You look beautiful," he said stepping inside and closing the door behind him.

He took her in his arms and inhaled the distinct aroma of the perfume she'd bought in the islands. "I know this may seem crazy. What started as a Christmas cruise caper has turned into so much more. I love you, Starr."

Her eyes widened and then she smiled, filling her green eyes with a light of excitement and a sheen of tears. "Oh, Noah. I love you too. Even when I was an elf, and you were Santa Claus."

Laughing at the images of them as spirits of Christmas, he cupped her face and kissed her, hoping to show her how much she meant to him. When they pulled apart, he took a box from his suit jacket and knelt in front of her.

"Starr, I know we have to resolve a few issues, but there's nothing we can't work out together. I want to spend the rest of my life with you. I know people will say I'm acting illogically, that love can't grow this fast, that deep, but they're wrong. I love you with all my heart and soul."

He opened the box and held it out to her. "Will you marry me?"

Starr clapped a hand to her mouth and nodded before throwing herself into his arms, tumbling them to the carpet. "Yes! Yes! I'll marry you."

Sitting up, facing one another, Noah slid a ring on her finger.

Starr stared at it, and frowning, turned to him. "Wait! This is Tara's ring."

The skin around his eyes crinkled with humor. "As we said goodbye, Tara slipped it into my pocket and told me to use it. We can pick out your real engagement ring together. In the meantime, this is the best I can do. It's the thought that counts, right?"

She smiled at him. "Such a wonderful thought. I love it and I love, love you."

He pulled her up to his feet and wrapped his arms around her, certain he'd made the best decision of his life. What had begun as a caper was turning into a Christmas dream come true.

# # #

Thank you for reading *A Christmas Cruise Caper*. If you enjoyed this book, please help other readers discover it by leaving a review on your favorite site. It's such a nice thing to do.

To stay in touch and to keep up with the latest news, here's a link to sign up for my periodic newsletter!
http://bit.ly/2OQsb7s

For your additional reading pleasure, please enjoy an excerpt from my Christmas Novella, *Holiday Hopes*.

CHAPTER ONE

Holly Winters left New York City relieved to have some time at home over the Christmas break, away from the turmoil of teaching English to juniors and seniors in high school. Her mother had made her promise to spend time in Ellenton, New York, with her, claiming it had been way too long since the two of them had had a Hallmark-type holiday together. She'd told Holly that she'd already baked and frozen cookies, had plenty of cocoa in the house, and movies ready to stream on her new television.

Ordinarily, Holly might've rolled her eyes at the suggestion, but it had been one year since her breakup with her boyfriend, and she was ready for "girl" time. She turned on holiday music on her car radio and hummed along. She loved the excitement, the music, the food, and hoped this holiday would be very different from the last when she'd been trying to recover from being dumped.

She'd almost reached the outskirts of Ellenton when her cell rang. She checked caller ID. *Katie Quinn*, her best friend from grammar school to the present day.

"Hey, Katie! What's up?"

"Holly, I'm in desperate need of your help. I've really messed things up this time."

"What now?" Katie always had a crisis of sorts.

"The last admin I placed at Devlin and Sons law firm, just up and quit. I have to find someone right away to replace her. I know you're on your way home, and you wouldn't have to stay at their office long. It's just until I find someone to replace you. Please, pretty please, help me."

"You know I'm here on a break from work, right?" Holly said, sighing.

"Yes, I'm aware of that, but remember when I moved to the city to be with you for an entire week after your breakup with Paul?"

Holly knew she had no choice. "Okay, I'll cover the assignment for you, but you'd better find someone to take my place in a hurry, or you'll have my mother to answer to. This was supposed to be our girl time."

"I'll make it up to both of you somehow," Katie said. "Call me when you get home and are settled. I'll fill you in with the details. And, Holly, I love you."

"Yeah, yeah," said Holly, knowing it was true. They were as close as any friends could be, more like sisters than friends.

Holly pulled into the driveway of the small Cape Cod house where she'd grown up and smiled when her mother rushed out the front door to greet her. They'd always been close, but then, they'd been forced to face the world together after her father unexpectedly died of a heart attack when she was only four.

Holly waved, got out of the car, and eagerly went into her mother's open arms. At fifty-two, Susan Winters was an attractive woman who worked in the maternity ward of the local hospital. The job suited her warm, caring personality.

"Home at last," said her mother. "I'm looking forward to having a few days off with you. I've sent out invitations to my annual Christmas Eve party and expect a nice crowd. Even added a few new people."

Holly cocked an eyebrow at her. "Do you mean young, single men?"

"Just a couple. It's been over a year since you and Paul broke up. It's time to move on." Her mother raised a hand to stop her. "Don't talk to me about being alone. I like it this way."

"Charlie Parker and you have been dating for years. Are you ever going to get married?"

Her mother laughed. "Probably not. At least for a while. We're best of friends, and that's how we like it. But you're young and have always wanted a big family of your own."

"That was before Paul. Now, I'm not sure. Hold on. I'll get my luggage and we can talk inside." Holly went to her car and took out the two suitcases she'd brought with her, glad she'd packed clothes that would be suitable for the temporary job she'd promised to Katie.

Her mother grabbed the handle of one of the suitcases and rolled it up to the front entrance. On either side of the front door, small Alberta spruce trees in pots were decorated with twinkling miniature white lights. A live green wreath with an enormous red bow hung on the door. Inside, Holly knew, a Christmas tree would be waiting for her to decorate with her mother. That was part of the fun of being home for the holidays.

Her mother ushered her inside and to the bedroom in the back of the house that had always been hers.

Holly studied her room, both amused and touched that her mother hadn't changed much about it since she'd left for college ten years ago. The soft-green paint on the walls was inviting and went well with the multi-colored quilt on her cherry, pencil-post bed. The desk she'd studied on in high school still sat in a nook, along with her desk chair. Above the desk was a bulletin board with photographs of various events, including a picture from her college graduation and a photo of Katie and her from high school days.

Seeing it, Holly turned to her mother. "Katie called and asked me for a favor. She needs someone to take over an administrative job at Devlin and Sons law firm, just until she can find a permanent replacement. I couldn't say no after all she did to lift my spirits after Paul and I broke up. I hope you don't mind. We'll still have our evenings together."

Her mother sighed. "I understand, but I hope Katie can find someone quickly. It's a difficult time of the year to be doing that."

Holly put an arm around her mother. "I'm not sure who I'll be working for, but it's all to help her."

"I've heard things haven't been the same there since Duncan Devlin passed. Such a shame. He was much too young to die. Just like your father, he dropped dead of a heart attack."

"I'm sorry. Who's taken his place? His son?"

"That's what I heard. I don't know much about him except he didn't grow up here but lived with his mother somewhere down south."

"Guess that's why I haven't met him," said Holly. "I'd left home by the time he moved here."

"He usually spends time away at the holidays, I understand, which is why he's never come to one of my parties," her mother said. "In fact, after being turned down a couple of times, I haven't sent him an invitation for this year."

"Well, I'll do my duty for Katie and spend the rest of the

time with you. I don't want to think of dating or getting involved with anyone here over the holidays. I'm happy with my life in the city."

"How are your little darlings? As cute and smart as always?"

Holly laughed. "It's a good group." Her darlings were rough high school kids who were a joy to teach once you got past the tough role they played. And, yes, some of them were adorable.

"I won't keep you from getting settled any longer," said her mother. "Meet me in the kitchen. I've made some wassail for us to have while decorating the tree."

Holly smiled. She definitely was home for the holidays.

She'd hung the last of her clothes in her closet when her phone rang. *Katie.*

Eager to hear details about the job she'd promised to take, Holly accepted the call.

"Hi, Holly," said Katie. "I've done more investigation into the reason my temp left the law firm and thought it fair that I give you a warning. She was working directly for Corey Devlin, the managing partner of the firm. Apparently, he can be quite demanding. In fact, she told me she was terrified of him. But, Holly, after handling your students, you should have no trouble. He used to be a lot of fun, easier to be around, but since his father died, he's changed. I think things will be fine if you go in there and be yourself."

"Hmmm. He sounds pretty bad, but I'll take care of him," said Holly, sounding more confident than she felt.

"He's going to be away for a couple of days which will give you time to see what the work is like and how you can help. He's left some work for you to do."

Holly paused and then blurted out, "What aren't you telling me? So far he sounds like a donkey."

"I've met him, and I like him. He just needs someone

strong to handle him. That's all I'm going to say. You'll figure him out very quickly. And in the meantime, I'll be looking for a replacement."

"Do you want to stop by this evening?" Holly asked.

"Thanks, but I have a date with Evan, but maybe tomorrow." Evan Whicker was the owner of an insurance agency and was a great guy. At one time, Holly had been attracted to him but quickly realized they were not well suited. She was highly organized. He was not. Katie and Evan together were perfect, and Katie was hopeful that Evan was about to give her an engagement ring.

"Ready to come trim the tree?" her mother asked, handing her a cup of the hot, cinnamon spicy liquid—her own recipe for old-fashioned wassail.

Holly took a sip and let out a soft murmur of delight. On this crisp, cold afternoon, it tasted delicious. She took off her boots and slipped into the fuzzy slippers she left in Ellenton for use and padded to the living room.

She glanced at the tall, round tree and inhaled the evergreen scent that emanated from it. "Smells good," she said. "Did Charlie put it up for you?"

Her mother smiled. "As always, the darling."

"Is he coming here tonight?" Holly asked. She thought Charlie was perfect for her mother and couldn't understand why they didn't get married. But each time she broached the subject, her mother shut her down.

"No, he's not. This is our time together. I've invited him for dinner tomorrow, though. He was almost as anxious to see you as I."

Holly looked at the neat cardboard boxes stacked on the floor. "Should we get started?"

Her mother raised her mug. "Yes! Here's to a wonderful holiday season. It's such a joy to be able to share it with you."

"Hear! Hear!" said Holly, gently clinking her mug against her mother's.

They set down their mugs and opened one of the boxes. Ornaments of all kinds were nestled inside. Her mother had collected special glass ornaments for years, and Holly felt like she was opening a gift each time she lifted one from the box.

Both Holly and her mother were fussy about displaying each ornament properly. They'd only finished one of the two boxes when the oven timer sounded.

"You go ahead and work on it. I'll check the casserole and put the rest of the dinner together," said her mother.

Holly nodded, lifted a little elf ornament, and hung it from a perfect branch up high in the tree. Satisfied with the way it looked, she stepped away and headed into the kitchen. She knew what her mother was having for dinner even before she smelled it.

A lemon chicken casserole was one of her favorites. That and a crisp, green lettuce salad was the perfect way to start off the visit.

Inside the kitchen, her mother served the casserole while Holly tossed the lettuce with a balsamic dressing.

Sitting at the table across from her mother, a sudden sting of tears startled Holly. Even though her family was small, she was happy to be home at the holidays and felt sorry for those who were alone at such a time.

Later, after the last ornament had been hung and the boxes put away, her mother announced she was going to bed.

Holly was happy to do the same. It had been a rough, few weeks at school, and she was ready to relax and rest. Then she remembered her commitment to Katie. She'd have to set the alarm clock because she couldn't be late to her new job.

About the Author

A *USA Today* **Best-Selling Author,** Judith Keim is a hybrid author who both has a publisher and self-publishes. Ms. Keim writes heart-warming novels about women who face unexpected challenges, meet them with strength, and find love and happiness along the way—stories with heart. Her best-selling books are based, in part, on many of the places she's lived or visited, and on the interesting people she's met, creating believable characters and realistic settings her many loyal readers love.

She enjoyed her childhood and young adult years in Elmira, New York, and now makes her home in Boise, Idaho, with her husband, Peter, and their lovable miniature Dachshund, Wally, and other members of her family.

While growing up, she was drawn to the idea of writing stories from a young age. Books were always present, being read, ready to go back to the library, or about to be discovered. All in her family shared information from the books in general conversation, giving them a wealth of knowledge and vivid imaginations.

Ms. Keim loves to hear from her readers and appreciates their enthusiasm for her stories.

"I hope you've enjoyed this book. If you have, please help other readers discover it by leaving a review on the site of your choice. And please check out my other books and series:

The Hartwell Women Series
The Beach House Hotel Series
The Fat Fridays Group
The Salty Key Inn Series
The Chandler Hill Inn Series
Seashell Cottage Books
The Desert Sage Inn Series
Soul Sisters at Cedar Mountain Lodge
The Sanderling Cove Inn Series
The Lilac Lake Inn Series

"ALL THE BOOKS ARE NOW AVAILABLE IN AUDIO on iTunes and other sites! So fun to have these characters come alive!"

Ms. Keim can be reached at **www.judithkeim.com**

And to like her author page on Facebook and keep up with the news, go to: **http://bit.ly/2pZWDgA**

To receive notices about new books, follow her on Book Bub:

https://www.bookbub.com/authors/judith-keim

"Sign up for my newsletter and get a free story. I keep my newsletters short and fun with giveaways, recipes, and the latest must-have news about me and my books. Welcome! Here's the link:

https://BookHip.com/RRGJKGN

"I am also on Twitter @judithkeim, LinkedIn, and Goodreads. Come say hello!"

Acknowledgements

As always, I am eternally grateful to my team of editors, Peter Keim and Lynn Mapp, my book cover designer, Lou Harper, and my narrator for Audible and iTunes, Angela Dawe. They are the people who take what I've written and help turn it into the book I proudly present to you, my readers! I also wish to thank my coffee group of writers who listen and encourage me to keep on going. Thank you, Peggy Staggs, Lynn Mapp, Cate Cobb, Nikki Jean Triska, Joanne Pence, Melanie Olsen, and Megan Bryce. And to you, my fabulous readers, I thank you f your continued support and encouragement. Without you, this book would not exist. You are the wind beneath my wings.